Linda Lee Welch is American but has lived most of her adult life in England. She is a working musician with her own band, a prize-winning poet, and an associate lecturer in Creative Writing at Sheffield Hallam University.

THE ARTIST OF EIKANDO

Junko Bayliss is a potter, famous for her exquisite designs. From the outside, she is seen as a successful, independent artist, but from the inside, Junko knows that her personal life is a mess. When her elegant but emotionally cold parents die only a few minutes apart, Junko is left to ponder the question marks that always hovered over her parents' lives, and their strange behaviour towards their only child. When her Aunt Helen hints at a mystery — something shocking that happened to Diane and Peter Bayliss during the Second World War — Junko decides to visit Japan, where her parents met, and hunt out their story . . .

LINDA LEE WELCH

THE ARTIST OF EIKANDO

Complete and Unabridged

ULVERSCROFT
Leicester

First published in Great Britain in 2004 by
Virago Press
an imprint of
Time Warner Book Group UK
London

First Large Print Edition
published 2005
by arrangement with
Time Warner Book Group UK
London

British Library CIP Data

Welch, Linda Lee
The artist of Eikando.—Large print ed.—
Ulverscroft large print series general fiction
1. Parent and adult child—Fiction
2. World War, *1939 – 1945*—Asia, Southeastern—
Fiction 3. Large type books
I. Title
813.6 [F]

ISBN 1–84395–852–X

Published by
F. A. Thorpe (Publishing)
Anstey, Leicestershire

Set by Words & Graphics Ltd.
Anstey, Leicestershire
Printed and bound in Great Britain by
T. J. International Ltd., Padstow, Cornwall

This book is printed on acid-free paper

The author gratefully acknowledges Penguin for permission to use extracts from *On Love and Barley: Haiku of Basho*, translated by Lucien Stryk, Penguin Classics © 1985, and *The Narrow Road to the Deep North and Other Travel Sketches* by Matsuo Basho, translated by Nobuyuki Yuasa, Penguin Classics © 1966.

This story is dedicated to the memory of
Sandra Dartnell (1944-2003).
That girl could sing.

Acknowledgements

I would like to thank the following people for their support: Yuji, Toshie, and Hideko Takahashi of Chiba, Japan, for their extra-special hospitality and kindness, and enduring friendship. Jesse, Maya, Yoichi, and Tennessee Glass, also of Chiba, for the same. Junko Matsui, for arranging my time at Meikai University, and helping to make it so delightful. Gill Goddard, of Sheffield University Library's Asian Studies Department.

Sandra Dartnell, Lesley Glaister, Jeff Horne, Andrew Madden, Christine O'Brien, Boo Spurgeon, Bob Welch, and James Whitford for invaluable input and advice.

Magical potter Penny Withers for her time, thoughts, and talent.

My editor at Virago, Antonia Hodgson, and my agent John Saddler, to both of whom I am eternally grateful.

Barbara Stanifoth, practice nurse, for medical advice.

As I was plodding along the River Fuji, I saw a small child, hardly three years of age, crying pitifully on the bank, obviously abandoned by his parents. They must have thought this child was unable to ride through the stormy waters of life which run as wild as the rapid river itself, and that he was destined to have a life even shorter than that of the morning dew. The child looked to me as fragile as the flowers of bush-clover that scatter at the slightest stir of the autumn wind, and it was so pitiful that I gave him what little food I had with me.

How is it indeed that this child has been reduced to this state of utter misery? Is it because of his mother who ignored him, or because of his father who abandoned him? Alas, it seems to me that this child's unde-served suffering has been caused by something far greater and more massive — by what one might call the irresistible will of heaven. If it is so, child, you must raise your voice to heaven, and I must pass on, leaving you behind.

The Records of a Weather-Exposed Skeleton,
Basho, trans. Nobuyuki Yuasa

Come, see real
flowers
of this painful world.

Basho, trans. Lucien Stryk

1

Junko stirred. As she opened her eyes she caught a whiff of the sheets tangled around her middle. They were sodden and reeking with sweat. The ceiling fan turned slowly above her head but the air-conditioning was off. Why had she done that? She couldn't remember.

She stared at the clock, which was winking at her. There must have been a power outage. Looking at the crack between the curtains, she figured it was either dawn or dusk. But what day? She had no idea, though she knew it was summer from the heat.

When the phone rang she recoiled. She didn't want to talk to anyone until she'd discerned the day and the hour, and how long her parents had been dead.

She was lying in her parents' bed. The headboard was teak, intricately carved with an oriental tale of love and loss. Junko had spent many childhood hours polishing the wood with an old toothbrush and lemon oil. She'd asked her mother a thousand times to tell her the story, but her mother had always said, *When you're older*. When Junko got older, her mother barely spoke to her at all.

The bedroom floor was covered with piles of clothes, shoes, books and papers. Junko could remember coming back here after the funeral and wandering the rooms. She had started to sort through her parents' belongings, but couldn't do it. She'd lain down with her battered copy of *Franny and Zooey*, which she always turned to in troubled times. That must have been days ago. The cheese and crackers on the bedside table were green with mould.

A sharp pang in her stomach caused her to double over. She was starving, and thirsty, and she needed to pee. Junko untangled herself from the sheets and limped to the bathroom. It took a full minute to empty her bladder. When she stood at the sink to wash her hands she caught sight of her face in the mirror. It was pale, almost white. There were dark circles under her eyes, which were bloodshot and so light blue they seemed invisible. Her long, wispy blond hair was matted and filthy. There was a glob of something, it looked like peanut butter, over her left ear. Junko groaned.

She made her way into the kitchen and opened the fridge. There wasn't much there, a few rotten tomatoes and a jug of iced tea. She looked in the freezer. There were six

Japanese-style TV dinners. Junko sighed, taking one out and turning the oven on. What she really wanted was a hot dog.

While her food was heating, Junko went to the front door and opened it. There were three newspapers lying on the lawn, wrapped in their plastic bags. *Three days*, she thought. *I've been asleep for three days.* But not wholly asleep. She could remember voices murmuring, bells ringing faintly, and seven ivory and wood and alabaster Buddhas sighing from their places on the shelf above her parents' bed.

She gathered the newspapers in her arms and took them to the kitchen table. Today must be Saturday, 2 June. That was the most recent *Houston Chronicle*. The funeral had been on Wednesday. God, it was hot. Junko fanned herself with the Lifestyle section and went to turn on the air-conditioning.

Junko Bayliss worked at the Lone Star Pottery in Montrose. She made and hand-painted jugs, plates and garden ceramics. She was well known for her minimalist, abstract designs. Her pots had been exhibited in New York and Los Angeles, and one critic had even given her style a name: Junkoesque. She had a little house in Montrose too, not far from the studio. But here she was at her childhood home in Clear Lake City, newly orphaned and not coping at all well, with peanut butter in her hair and a terrible howl building up in her heart.

The oven buzzed. Junko turned it off and lifted her dinner out. It was getting darker and the wall clock in the kitchen said seven-thirty, so it must be dinner. As she sat down at the table the phone rang again. She picked it up, her mouth full of teriyaki. 'Hello?'

'June. Are you all right, dear? Only I've been phoning for days.' It was Aunt Helen, calling from Kemah. Aunt Helen was Junko's only living relation now, her mother's sister. Helen had always been kind to Junko, in a pitying kind of way. *Poor thing*, she used to murmur as she patted the child's fair head. As Junko grew into a successful artist, Helen's sighing over her abated, and they became close. Junko adored her aunt, truly; but being in Helen's company could still sometimes make her squirm slightly, as if she were about to fall and graze her knee.

'I'm fine, Aunt Helen. Just very tired.' Aunt Helen said nothing. 'There's a lot to do.' Junko filled the silence with the obvious.

'Can I help? Really, I'd like to help.'

'Come on over if you want. But give me an hour or so, OK? I need to clean up.'

8

'You don't need to clean for me,' her aunt chided.

'I mean clean myself up. I'm a red-hot mess.'

'All right, sugar, I'll see you in an hour.'

As she placed the phone in its cradle Junko groaned again. She could use some help, that was for sure. But what she wanted most of all was to walk right out of here, into some cool and soothing foreign landscape where nothing was familiar.

The Bayliss house was a ranch-style, four-bedroom place, facing west, in its own acre of ground. There were two fat palm trees in the front yard, on either side of the driveway. Out back was a large deck, covered with plants of various shapes and sizes in exotic pots, mostly oriental. Junko's designs were not among them.

Inside there was a formal front room just beyond the entryway, and a large kitchen along the whole north side of the house, which led into the family room at the back. The bedrooms were off a hallway on the south side. One of them had been hers for eighteen years, although no trace of Junko could be found in it now. Her mother had converted it into a sewing room when Junko left home for art school. When Junko came home for Christmas in her freshman year, she

9

was surprised to find her belongings in boxes in the loft. She slept on the couch in the family room, and didn't come home for the holidays again. Diane and Peter Bayliss didn't mind. On the rare occasions that Junko did see her folks after that, they always looked vaguely surprised, as if they couldn't quite remember her name.

Junko made her way back to the master bedroom, where she'd left her overnight case. She hadn't brought a change of clothes. She'd take a shower and see if she could find something of Diane's that would fit. It'd have to be shorts or a skirt; Junko was six inches taller than her mother.

The shower was Junko's favourite place in her parents' house. It was powerful, and hit her hard and steaming. She would stay in it for hours as a child, until her mother made her get out. She stepped in now and turned it on, then waited for the water to get hot. There was some shampoo on the shelf, and soap in a dish. Her mother's shower cap hung on a hook beside the sink. Everything in its place, as usual. Except them. Through the noise of the water Junko could hear the Buddhas humming, and she hummed along with them as she scrubbed her hair and body clean.

Junko had always seen things no one else

could see. The cicadas spoke a language only she could understand. Inanimate Buddhas sang to her when she was blue and dislocated, and seemed to drift above their stations, but only when her parents weren't looking. She saw Jesus walk across the moon when she was six. She made the mistake of mentioning this to her mother, who shook her head sadly and told Junko to think about what happened to bad little girls who told lies.

After that, Junko kept her visions to herself.

She'd been ill from too many mosquito bites after spending a day on Armand Bayou with her mother. Nothing serious, but she was dizzy and shocked for a few days. Her mother had seemed frightened of coming near her, like she might catch the itch or something, little Junko had thought at the time. So she spent the days and nights alone, trying not to scratch, and staring out of her bedroom window. On one of those nights she saw, as plain as anything, a silhouette of Jesus walking across the face of the moon, holding a candle in front of him. It was wonderful.

⋆ ⋆ ⋆

She was looking through her mother's closet when she heard the doorbell ring. Junko

11

grabbed a bathrobe and threw it on as she headed for the door. Aunt Helen stood on the porch with some cuttings from her ginger plant in one hand and a sweet-potato pie in the other. She was dressed in her usual flowing kaftan, her long grey hair done up in a twisted knot. Aunt Helen was beautiful.

'I thought you might be hungry, June.' Helen made her way into the kitchen and put the pie on the table. She opened the back door and put the cuttings in the utility room.

'Starved,' Junko replied, indicating the half-eaten TV dinner and getting a knife from the drawer. 'Want some?'

'No, dear. I've got another one at home. You eat it up.' Helen's soft Southern lilt was one of Junko's favourite sounds, and she felt her eyes fill up. She gulped. But the tears were running now. Aunt Helen put her arms around Junko and squeezed.

'Let 'em come, June-bug, just you go ahead and let 'em come.' Junko rested her head on her aunt's shoulder and wept. Her appetite had vanished.

Later, they sat outside under the mimosa tree and watched the stars. 'How did they do it? I mean, *how*?' Junko whispered into the night.

'It's uncanny, isn't it? To die like that, within minutes of each other, when both seemed so well.' Helen smoked her cigarette. 'They *were* both seventy-five, I guess . . . ' Helen's voice trailed off. 'They were very close.'

'Tell me about it.' Junko almost spat the words. Helen took her hand.

'It wasn't about you, I mean about who you are, honey.'

'What was it about?' Junko asked. 'I'd really like to know.'

'Something must have happened, way before you were born.' Helen shook her head. 'She was different, after the war, I mean. Diane came back a different woman.' She leaned forward and looked into Junko's face. 'I swear it, they never told me what it was. They never did, or I'd tell you now. I swear it, June.'

'I know. It's OK.' Junko swatted at a mosquito. 'I think he tried to tell me once, you know. I was real little, though — Ouch!' She slapped her bare calf. 'Little beasts! I'm getting eaten alive out here.' Junko hated mosquitoes with a rare passion, and sometimes wondered why in the world she'd stayed in Texas.

'Aunt Helen?'

'What, hon?'

'Did you miss Uncle Deke for long after he died?'

Helen laughed softly. 'Still miss him now. But it was a done deal, June. He was forty years older, and from the day I married him I was preparing to lose him. Didn't think it would happen quite so quick, though.' She shook her head. 'I was just twenty-seven years old.'

'You never . . . I mean, no man was . . . '

'I like my company. Didn't need that passion again.'

Junko stared at the sky. At nearly thirty-six, she'd never felt any passion for a man at all, never mind the kind that could sustain you, in its absence, for forty years. She glanced at her aunt. 'Want to go on in?'

'Might as well make a start.'

They got up from their chairs. Junko folded them and put them back in the garage, just as her mother would have done, then followed her aunt into the house. They had a lot to do.

* * *

Junko hauled the last box out the front door and into the van. Sweat was dripping from every pore of her skin as she signed the driver's form. This was her parents' life, all packed up and double wrapped where necessary, about to make its way to auction and beyond. The bedstead story she'd never

14

know now, the thousand and one *cloisonné* vases and salt cellars, the silkscreen prints and sandalwood fans. She hadn't kept much: one of the seven Buddhas, the smallest, ivory one. A plant pot. There were no photographs.

She slunk back into the empty house feeling as empty as it was, hollowed out. It seemed peculiar to be missing something she'd never really had, but she was. Grief bubbled away, evaporating her strength. She hadn't been to work in three weeks, and she wasn't anywhere near being ready to return. Junko slid down the living-room wall and sat on the floor. She needed to go home and check her mail, but she could hardly move.

The phone rang.

Junko moved towards it as if through mud. She picked up the receiver and said, 'Yes?' just as her mother would have done, startling herself. A woman's voice came over the crackling line, '*Konichiwa*, Diane.'

'No. I mean, this isn't Diane. This is her daughter. Diane died three weeks ago.' Junko's parents went every year to Japan, but she didn't know they had friends there. She didn't know what to say. 'Can I . . . '

'Daughter?' The caller was obviously surprised.

'Yes. This is Junko Bayliss.'

The woman gasped. 'Junko?'

15

'Who is this?' Junko was suddenly desperate to know.

'So sorry, sorry,' the woman mumbled and hung up.

Junko stood with the receiver at her ear. She felt as if her heart had stopped. Here was a clue, something solid and alive, that might lead her to her parents' past.

Suddenly she could see herself at Houston International Airport, queuing for JAL. She was going to Japan. She'd gather her inheritance and do some travelling.

2

'Hey, Junie. How you doing?' Billy looked up over the rims of his reading glasses, a real question in his voice. He was studying a series of watercolours. The Lone Star Pottery displayed paintings and sculptures too, mainly to support local artists. Billy's long grey hair was braided into a single plait, and his beard was trimmed short and neat. He was sixty, and looked it, and loved it. He had four grown-up kids who all came home for Christmas, and a wife who played viola for the Houston Symphony Orchestra. He was always a little bit concerned about Junko, who seemed to have no one.

Junko sat down on the canvas chair beside Billy. 'Good enough,' she replied with a worn-out smile. Billy raised his eyebrows.

'Yeah?'

'Yeah. Really. The house deal's done. I signed this morning.'

'Feel funny?'

'Some,' Junko said, 'but I'll get over it.' She was looking at the picture in Billy's hands. It was of a park just down the road from where she grew up, where the jungle gyms were all

17

modelled on spaceships and the swings were shaped like stars. She remembered playing there often as a child, with her mother sitting on a bench, staring into the trees as if a message would emerge from them, or a Martian, or a thief.

'When you off?'

'Tomorrow morning. The flight's at ten.'

'Direct to Tokyo?'

'LA, Hawaii, Tokyo. About nineteen hours in all.'

'Remember to keep wiggling your toes.'

Junko nodded affectionately and reached to touch the back of Billy's hand. 'I'm going to miss you.' She felt her cheeks redden, and pulled herself up from the chair. Billy stood too, and took her in his embrace, and held her there until she relaxed into it.

'You stay in touch, hear? I don't want to be losing sleep worrying about where you are.' Billy held her at arm's length now. 'You look tired. I guess you can sleep on the plane.'

She nodded. 'I'm just going to clear up my stuff.' She made her way to the small workroom at the back of the gallery. She'd been here for all of her working life, and leaving felt like tearing off her skin. But she'd be back, wouldn't she? When she found whatever it was she needed to find.

In fact, there was nothing to clear up at all.

Everything — the paints and brushes, the glazes and cloths and tools — was packed away in the cupboard where she'd left it. Junko ran her finger along the worktop. So many pots she'd made and painted here, the clay and water mixed and spun, baked and burned. Earth and water and fire and air, that was her world. She turned and walked back to Billy's table.

'For you,' he said, holding out a hand-worked clay St Christopher medal, the size of a quarter, strung on a thin leather thong. 'Patron saint of travellers. Made it myself.' Junko put the necklace on.

'Thanks, Billy.' She held the medal to her chest. 'Thank you.'

'Take good care.'

She gave him a final hug and stepped out into the muggy heat, heading home. She'd finish packing first, then get some dinner from the Hot Dog Shop.

★　★　★

Junko's neighbour Gloria Gonzales was waiting for her when she got home, sitting on the front steps reading a magazine. Gloria's huge leather bag was lying beside her on the porch, overflowing with sunglasses, scarves, books, pens in a variety of colours. 'Didn't

19

want to miss you,' she said as Junko climbed out of her car. 'I'm going to the show in Hermann Park later on. The whole clan's coming! We'll probably just about fill the place. Mama's making one of her gargantuan picnics.' Gloria paused for breath. 'You want to move those plants now? Or in the morning?' She was taking care of the houseplants while Junko was away.

'Now's good. Come on in.' Gloria was five-foot-nothing, with vivid black hair and eyes, and made June feel like a ghostly giant. 'Did you get Aunt Helen's ginger in?' Junko asked as she unlocked the door.

'Yep. I put it along the fence at the back. Perfect.' They walked through the front room and into the kitchen.

'I was kinda worried I'd left it in the bag for too long.'

'It's tough stuff, Junie. Like you.' Gloria lifted her mop of hair off her neck and wafted it like a fan. 'You all set?'

'Nearly. Coffee?' Gloria nodded. 'I've just got to pack my toothbrush and pick a few books to take with me.' Junko got the coffee maker going and sat down next to Gloria. 'I can't believe I'm going. Doesn't seem real yet.'

'You'll have a blast. I'd love to see Japan. It must be so — so — foreign! Take lots of pictures, OK?'

'I don't have a camera.'

'Oh yes you do.' Gloria reached into her bag and produced a small Canon. She handed it to Junko with a grin. 'Going-away present.'

'Gloria!' Junko felt a blush prickling her scalp. She wasn't used to unexpected gifts, and getting two in one day was almost unbearable.

To Junko it seemed that she had walked through her life up till now with one leg missing. Nobody noticed; at least, nobody said anything. But she felt off-balance and aggrieved, and missing at least five toes' worth of grip on the ground. Moments like this confused her. They challenged her notion of herself as *other*, a non-player on the home team.

She placed the camera on the table and poured coffee into cups.

'Send me some shots of you and Mount Fuji.'

'I will.'

'So,' Gloria drank her coffee, 'what do you know?'

'An address in Kyoto. That's all I found. A woman called Hiromi Mitsuki.'

'Have you called her?'

'Uh-uh.' Junko shook her head. 'I'm not even sure . . . ' Her voice trailed off.

'Oh come on, Junie. You deserve to know whatever it is there is to know.' She peered at her friend. 'If you want to, of course. But it's your whole life we're talking about here.'

'It must have been Hiromi Mitsuki who called that day. Hers was the only Japanese address in my parents' files. She was so shocked when I told her who I was she couldn't speak.' Bodey, Junko's ginger tomcat, jumped on to her lap. Junko scratched his ears. 'Bye-bye, butterball.' She hugged him to her chest and looked at Gloria. 'She'll probably turn me away. I don't know if I could take that.'

'It's a risk — '

'I know it.'

'But Junie — '

'I'll try. OK? I'll try.'

'Honey, I don't want you to get yourself hurt, you know that.'

Junko nodded.

'Anyway,' Gloria sighed, 'Bodey will be fine with me. Plenty of opossums around here to keep him busy. And we'll all be waiting for you when you get home.'

Home, Junko thought. *Strange notion. I guess home is where the cat is.*

3

Diane Winkler grew up in Athens, Texas, one of two daughters of schoolteacher parents. Her mother was forty-three when she found herself pregnant for the first time. Hilda and Vern Winkler had given up hope of a child, and were delighted when Diane was born. They didn't spoil her or mollycoddle; she was treated to the same education as every other child in their one-room schoolhouse, as was her sister Helen, who arrived exactly a year later.

Diane was a serious, dreamy child. She loved her folks, but when the war came along she was determined to do something, so in 1943 she left her job with the Post Office and joined the WACS. She started out in Virginia and ended up on Okinawa in June 1945. She'd never seen so many pineapples in her life.

The turquoise sea, the perpetual, gaudy hibiscus flowers, and victory in sight, made for a charged and intense time. At a dance one night Diane met Peter Bayliss.

'Martini?' he asked, handing her a glass. The tiny onion in the bottom glimmered like a pearl. 'Where you from?'

'Athens,' she smiled.

His eyes widened.

'Athens, Texas.'

'How exotic!'

She laughed. 'Not really.'

'Oh yes,' he nodded. 'Dance?'

Diane put her glass down on the nearest table and he swept her away. A week later they were inseparable. They were delirious. They couldn't wait, and made love on the beach with their toes in the surf, without protection.

'Marry me?' Peter whispered into her salty neck.

'Oh yes,' she replied.

They planned the wedding with the base chaplain. It would be in two weeks' time. They sent telegrams to family and letters to friends, and waited impatiently.

★   ★   ★

By the end of that June, all of Okinawa was in American hands. Peter was out on patrol with six other men one roaring hot July afternoon when they came across a group of women tending their vegetable patch.

'Whoopee!' Twenty-two-year-old Steven Marshall from Delaware threw his hat in the

24

air. 'Let's go!' He and two others charged towards the terrified women, who turned and ran for their lives. The men caught hold of the slowest girl and pushed her to the ground.

Potter and Majinski knelt on her arms while Marshall cut the sash from around her kimono with a knife he pulled from his belt. He opened the dress and slashed neatly up the front of her underskirt, whistling 'Old MacDonald' as he did so. The other two were pinching her nipples and kneading her breasts. Majinski spat several times on his hand and rubbed it in. The girl was mute with horror; she looked no more than fourteen or fifteen years old.

'What the hell are you doing?' Peter lurched towards them. He'd heard some wicked things, but had never witnessed any. Certainly he'd never been a part of so gross an act of misconduct, if that was what this was called. The three men around him were looking away. Marshall had his dick in his hand now, getting it ready. Potter, on Marshall's right, cast a menacing look in Peter's direction. Marshall glanced briefly at Peter and then thrust hard into the tiny girl's trembling frame.

'These aren't PEOPLE,' he panted in rhythm with his work. 'For CHRIST's sake, THIS, is the ENEMY. You some PANSY or

WHAT, WHAT, WHAT?' Marshall groaned and rolled off, spent.

For the first time the girl made a sound, something between a whimper and a moan. As the second soldier got ready for his turn she seemed to pass out.

Peter turned away and blanched. He felt stupefied and sick. And utterly, utterly helpless. He saw a cricket hopping through the grass and heard its song. His vomit narrowly missed it.

Junko was her name, not that anyone had stopped to ask. When the boys finished, Marshall gave Junko a kick in the ribs. She tried to turn and crawl away but Marshall forced her back and, with a final thrust and swipe, cut her throat. He cleaned his blade by jamming it into the ground several times and then wiping it on his pants.

'Let's go.' Marshall headed off, whistling again. Peter stumbled behind.

4

There's a seventy-year-old woman living in Kyoto with a fifty-year-old child. The woman is a potter. They live in the grounds of Eikando Temple. The child — for that is what he is — sweeps leaves from the paths in autumn and dust from the tatami all year round.

Toshie and Yuji enjoy their simple life. They are devout Buddhists. The umbilical cord was wrapped tightly twice around Yuji's neck when he was born and he went for just that little bit too long without a full supply of oxygen, which led to mild brain damage. His is a world of the senses, and the sublime. He is much loved by Toshie, who is not his mother. He is in control of his bodily functions, and can speak using simple language, but doesn't much; he'd rather listen.

Together they are waiting for something to happen. They're not sure what, but they know it's coming.

5

Junko arrived at Narita Airport in a daze of missed sleep and confusion. She'd been held up in LA due to a bomb scare, and nearly missed her flight to Hawaii. In Honolulu they'd sat on the runway for an hour before being invited off the plane and then back on to another one.

At the luggage carousel, she was aware that people were staring at her. She was at least a head taller than most, and her blond hair seemed to flash like neon. She grabbed her bag and crawled through Customs, emerging eventually into the fug of a Tokyo summer afternoon. She'd read somewhere that Mount Fuji was visible only 5 per cent of the time from the city due to its incredible output of smog.

Junko took a bus to Tokyo Station, where she would need to find the platform for the Kyoto *shinkansen*, the bullet train. She'd bought a Japanese Rail card in Houston, which would entitle her to travel anywhere she wanted in the country for two weeks. The incredible sprawl of the city rolled by her, its concrete and chrome gleaming in the August heat. There were colourful billboards and signs, which all seemed to be exclaiming something! But it was all Greek to Junko, or rather, Japanese. The gaudy characters looked more like decorations for her pots than letters. It was scary, being utterly unable to access the language. She felt a wave of terror shoot up her spine. What was she doing here?

As the bus got further into town, she saw words she recognized, written in English: Mitsubishi, Microsoft, McDonald's. Somehow this made her feel worse.

At the station, people seemed to be flying in all directions, charging up and down stairs clutching briefcases, shopping bags, mobile phones, children and lunchboxes. Luckily the train schedules were written in English as well as Japanese, so it was a fairly straightforward effort to locate the right train. Navigating the throng was tricky, and Junko nearly went flying herself when a young salaryman (she'd have sworn he wasn't a day older than twelve) ran past her with his briefcase flapping. It caught the back of her leg, but she managed to right herself OK.

Junko hadn't spoken a word to anyone yet, except the bus driver. She felt like she had a rock in her mouth and couldn't move it.

'English?' The young woman seated by the window smiled as Junko was stowing her bag.

'American,' Junko mumbled, taking her seat.

'Which state?' she asked. She was a tiny, fine-boned creature, and reminded Junko of the hummingbirds back home, all flutter and brightness and buzzing with intent.

She swallowed hard, but her throat stayed dry. 'Texas.'

'Ah.' The woman nodded her head. 'My father goes to Houston on business. I've seen pictures.'

'Your English is very good!' Junko was amazed that the first conversation she was having with a stranger in Japan would be with an English-speaking person who had connections to Houston.

'I'm Hideko.' She made a little bow, a swift nod of her head. 'My father taught us English from very early. He says it's the language of commerce.' She grinned. 'I want to be an artist! But it has been useful.'

'I'm an artist. Junko,' she said, 'that's my name.'

'Junko! How did you get Junko?'

'My parents loved Japan. I guess . . . I never really asked. I guess they just liked the name.' She had asked her mother, just once, and her mother had sighed and left the room. She'd never found the courage to ask again, and anyway, everybody called her June.

'Are you a painter?' Hideko asked.

'A potter. But I paint a lot of my pots.'

'Ah, so. I paint people, and scenes. I have a studio in my parents' home. My teacher comes once a week. My father arranged it.'

Junko nodded. She didn't know what to say. The seats were wide and comfortable, and she leaned her head back.

'Where are you going? To Kyoto? Sightseeing? Alone?'

Junko nodded again. 'A break . . . ' Her voice trailed off. She cleared her throat. 'I'm taking a break.'

'How long will you stay in Kyoto?'

'Well, I'm not sure. I've booked a room for a week at the Kyoto Royal Hotel. After that . . . ' She shrugged, looking out at the wooded hills. She hadn't expected Japan to be so mountainous.

Hideko leaned eagerly towards her. 'Can I paint you? Would you mind?'

Just then the train hurtled into a tunnel. Junko waited until they'd come out the other end before replying. 'Me?' She was stunned. 'But, why me?'

'There isn't anyone else in Kyoto who looks like you, I think so!' Hideko's laugh was a tinkling thing, like tiny bells. It made Junko smile. 'And my father would like to meet you, I'm sure.'

31

Hideko's enthusiasm was irresistible. 'How much time would you need? I mean, how many sittings? Only I'm just not — I don't know for sure what I'm going to be doing. Exactly.' Junko shivered slightly, and crossed her arms across her chest for warmth. The coach was air-conditioned, which she hadn't been expecting either. What had she been expecting, she wondered?

'Only one time. Then my mind and memory do the rest. That's how I've been taught.'

'OK, then,' Junko agreed, thinking, *What the hell am I doing?*

They went through more mountain tunnels at Odawara, passed Atami with its steep slopes of climbing houses, saw snow-capped mountains at Shin-Fuji, but not Fuji-san itself. Hamamatsu's huge, sparkling lake was crowded with boats and fish farms. Toyohashi looked like the vegetable capital of the world, with acres of polytunnels and greenhouses. Nagoya's centre was all office blocks and gleaming windows. As they rolled through Maibara, Hideko gave Junko her address. They'd arranged to meet the next day in the Gion district, at the Tsujiri Tearoom.

★ ★ ★

32

That night, Junko sat at the table in her room wearing the *yukata* provided by the hotel for sleeping in. Its wide blue and white stripes reminded her of the beach umbrella her parents took with them on their trips to Galveston. She recalled being about ten, lying in the umbrella's shade with the Gulf breeze caressing her already long, lean form. Her parents always seemed somewhat embarrassed at her size. By the age of fifteen, she was already five-foot-eleven, an inch taller than her father. A freak.

On these infrequent days out, Junko would swim and read, swim and doze, while her parents sat holding hands and gazing out to sea, as if trying to discern some secret in the scribbling surf.

She wrote a postcard to Gloria.

Hey, Glory,

My eyes are closing as I write. But wanted you to know I'M HERE. Kyoto. The other side of the world. Beautiful place, surrounded by green hills, an almost mystical feel about it. But very modern too. Will keep you informed.

Scratch Bodey for me, OK? Tomorrow I'll take pictures!

June

She crawled into bed and thought, as she drifted off, *Weird. Come to Kyoto and end up an artist's model.* The thought, and the memory of Hideko's enchanting laughter, sent her smiling to sleep.

6

The Gion district, with its flapping red and white flags, was a curious mish-mash of styles and customs. There were traditional geishas clip-clopping along in their elaborate kimonos and white faces. Modern geishas were elegant and stylish, dressed in Western designer wear and smelling like tantalizing exotic flowers. Junko had to remember to keep her mouth closed. More than once she found herself gaping at the sheer perfection of these women.

The Tsujiri Tearoom was packed. Hideko was already seated when Junko arrived. She'd left instructions with the girl tending the line of waiting customers to usher Junko in to her table; Junko wasn't hard to spot in these surroundings.

'*Konichiwa*, Junko.'

'Hello,' Junko answered, glancing at the menu in front of her. Everything on it was green! There were pictures of all that was on offer, and all of it varied from chartreuse to olive drab. She looked at Hideko, who laughed delightedly at the look on Junko's face.

'It's a special green-tea place. Everything, green tea. Green-tea noodles, green-tea tofu, green-tea jelly, green-tea ice-cream with green-tea sauce! OK?'

'Oh my my,' Junko said, picturing her usual chilli-cheese-dog meal. 'This is wild.'

'Very delicious too. And very healthy, of course.'

'What are you having?'

'First, noodles. Then ice-cream and jelly.'

'I'll go with you.' Junko closed her menu and blinked. She looked around her. It was a small place, on two levels and so crowded the waitresses had to squeeze their way around. Hideko and Junko were on the top floor.

'How is your hotel?'

'Fine, thanks. Very comfortable. The breakfast buffet kinda threw me, though. The *mirinboshi* was incredible, but I think I'd rather eat it later in the day.'

'Ah, so! You are very brave, Junko. Not many Americans I think would try *mirinboshi* for breakfast. They had cornflakes too?'

'Never did like cornflakes.' Junko was picturing the fat Tokyo businessman who'd sat next to her that morning. He'd been eating a huge bowl of cornflakes, milk dripping down his chin. She'd asked him what her food was called, and he'd explained: 'A delicacy. Flattened white-bait soaked in saki, then grilled, covered in sesame seeds.'

Hideko ordered and the food arrived quickly. They ate in friendly silence. Junko thought, *I'm probably old enough to be her mother!* She asked, 'How old are you, Hideko?'

'Twenty next month. Getting old!' she tinkled. 'Would you like me to show you around this afternoon?'

'Umm . . . I've got some things to do . . . thanks so much. There's something I need to do first. Maybe tomorrow?'

'OK, fine by me. I'll come to the Royal at 10 a.m. Meet me in the lobby? And maybe tomorrow we can decide the sitting day?'

'Good.' Junko smiled. She'd smiled more smiles in the last two days than she had in months.

7

Zenrin-ji is the head temple of the Japanese Buddhist sect Jodo Shu, or Pure Land Buddhism. The sect was founded in AD 855 by Shinsho. People call the temple Eikando after its seventh and most famous head priest, Eikan.

On 15 February 1082, Eikan was in the main hall of the temple chanting *nembutsu*, walking around and around the altar. Suddenly, Amida Buddha climbed down from the altar and started to walk ahead of Eikan, who was so astonished that he stopped on the spot. Amida looked over his left shoulder at Eikan and admonished, 'Eikan! You're dawdling!'

Eikan was so affected by this event that he commissioned a sculpture of Amida Buddha looking over his shoulder. This statue, called *Mikaeri-Amida*, became, and remains, the central object of worship at Eikando. It is said that this backwards glance is of great comfort to the wayward, the misguided, the stragglers of this life.

People come from all over to visit Eikando. It is especially beautiful at night, when lanterns are lit along the winding paths that lead up the slopes and through the maples. The main hall itself is magnificent, snuggled into the hillside, framed by the trees, its guyed tower straining towards heaven.

Hiromi Mitsuki has worked in the Eikando gift shop for fifty years. She was twenty when she started, in 1945, after the big bombs. She sells lucky charms and trinkets, and cards and pictures of Amida Buddha. Her husband, Kenichiro, sells tea and soba noodles in the grounds of the temple. They have four grown children who all live in Kyoto with their own families.

People come to Hiromi with burdens, troubles, confessions of all sorts. Her tranquil nature and sweet smile invite confidences. She has the aura of a healer about her. At seventy, she hasn't a single grey hair, and could easily be mistaken for forty.

Before they had children of their own, Hiromi and Kenichiro were involved in the fostering of a newborn baby. The child was simple, but Hiromi cherished him. She took him to work with her every day until she fell pregnant with her own child, at which time she placed him permanently in the care of Toshie the potter. She still sees him most days. Little Yuji has grown up with a temple for a home, and a loving and devoted extended family of Eikando monks and workers.

8

Junko was dreaming. She was at her wheel in Houston, but then the location shifted and she found herself on the side of a hill overlooking a broad, sparkling plain. The pot she was making was very large, and growing. Panic set in as she realized that she wasn't kicking any more, but the wheel was spinning faster and faster. The pot was now as big as Junko. She woke up gasping for air, feeling suffocated and terrified. She rose from her bed and got a drink of water, and sat down, dazed, at the little table by the window. The bright white lights of the Marion Hotel across the road seemed real enough. It was 3 a.m.

She'd gone to Eikando that afternoon and wandered around. The atmosphere of the place was serene and majestic. Junko had sat on a stone step and contemplated her mission here. What did she want? An explanation? A revelation of who she was and why? It was highly doubtful that anyone she might meet here could answer her questions, let alone define her life for her. What on earth had she been thinking? Best just see the sights and not interfere in anyone else's troubles. This place was about her parents' lives, not hers.

The address she'd found in her parents' house was just 'Hiromi Mitsuki, Eikando Temple, Kyoto'. Junko opened her notebook to the page where she'd written the address and ripped it out, crumpled it up and threw it in the bin. It would be gone in the morning after the maid came in to clean.

She crawled into bed and lay there, exhausted but sleepless. She remembered lying in her bed as a child, wishing so hard on the stars she could see out of her window that her fists and jaw would clench with the effort. Junko wished, she wished for once to be on the inside of the story looking out with her mother and father, instead of being always outside looking in.

Something had happened, Aunt Helen said. Her father had said something similar once, but never finished the story. With Junko, it was different: something hadn't happened. Something that should have, that was as necessary as breathing, simply hadn't happened, and she'd been left to figure out for herself about inhale, exhale, keep it steady. Well, she'd done it, hadn't she? And now they were gone.

How can you go on needing something that's gone, if it was never really there in the first place?

Diane and Peter had both been thirty-nine when Junko was born. Maybe she'd been an unlucky accident, although neither had actually said so. Certainly, Junko had grown up with the feeling that she should apologize for something, something grievous and terrible. The trouble was, she was pretty much a model child. She spoke quietly and — by the age of ten, anyway — only when spoken to. She did well in school, and showed artistic talent from an early age. She never asked for birthday parties or to have friends around. She was careful to be no trouble to her folks. But they didn't even notice that.

Junko's best friend in grade school was Mary Ann Foster. Junko spent many a happy afternoon at Mary Ann's house. Her mother, Mary Lynne, was always baking something sweet, and was usually covered in a dusting of flour, with her wiry hair sticking out wildly from under the headscarf that was meant to contain it. The house was chaos, with five children coming and going and coming again. Junko loved it. She loved the dust in the corners and the dog and the cat and the freedom to laugh out loud whenever you wanted to.

When Mary Ann and Junko started high school, they drifted apart. Junko spent her lunchtimes and breaks in the art room. Her teacher, Mrs Carney, encouraged her right from the start. Junko was grateful for Mrs Carney's attention; it was benign and mostly silent, and she provided Junko with all the materials she wanted. When it became apparent in the tenth grade that pottery was going to be Junko's thing, Mrs Carney pestered the school into buying a new potter's wheel. Her investment paid off: Junko won a scholarship to Columbia University and had her first major exhibition in New York City at the tender age of twenty-two. Mrs Carney came up from Houston for the opening. Junko's parents did not.

Junko turned and closed her eyes and thought about her dream. What if she'd let it happen, just let the pot spin and grow until it engulfed her or included her in its design? She was a coward, she could see that now. She should have seen it through.

Sick on a journey —
over parched fields
dreams wander on.

Basho, trans. Lucien Stryk

9

Peter told Diane about the rape. He started in a dry, factual tone and ended with a sob. Diane held him. 'It wasn't you, Pete. There was nothing you could have done to stop it.' She smoothed the silky brown hair back off his brow. She could see the beginnings of furrows there, though he was only twenty-five and had so far escaped any serious action in this war. He had a degree in economics, and had joined the Army to fight, but had been put to work in Supply. He'd been in Washington DC until coming to the South Pacific.

'Let's think about the future, sweetheart. This war will be over soon,' Diane went on. 'Can we live in Texas? Or do you want to go home to California?'

Peter had worked for a big accounting firm in San Francisco after finishing Berkeley. He wanted to set up his own financial consulting business, and could do that anywhere, as long as there were clients to be had. His two brothers were both in Chico, near their mother. His dad died of a stroke soon after Peter, the youngest, was born. Peter's mom never really got over it, and didn't have much time or affection for the baby of the family. His brothers brought him up, and didn't do a bad job. But he wasn't very close to them now.

'How about Houston?' he asked, squeezing her hand. 'We could get to Athens when we needed to.'

'Great! Helen and Deke are in Kemah now. And I've got a good friend in Pearland. Molly Greengrass. You'll love her.' She kissed Peter's forehead. 'Wars bring out the worst in some folks. But I guess those people might be acting the same way at home. They just get an excuse in wartime.'

'This war's done me the biggest favour of my life so far.' Peter spoke intensely. 'I've found you. And in three days, it'll be official.'

The wedding was all set to go.

★ ★ ★

The next morning Diane was delivering mail. It was a beautiful day, and she was dawdling. She went around to the back of a Quonset hut where three Okinawan men were waiting. They were employed by the US Army, but were about to quit. One of them was Junko's brother, one was her cousin. The third was her friend.

'Hi,' Diane smiled. The smile hadn't faded when the gag went on and the bag went over her head. The men placed her on the floor of the Jeep they were driving and left the base. They drove into the hills and got their revenge. They didn't kill her, but left her bleeding and vanished into Okinawa's remote interior.

It took a couple of hours for alarm bells to sound. Diane hadn't met Peter for lunch as they'd planned, but he'd assumed she'd been busy. The workmen weren't discovered missing until they failed to return the Jeep at the end of the day. When it became clear that something was wrong, a search was organized. Peter found Diane first. She was crawling along the road in the twilight, in pain and in shock. She was heading in the wrong direction, into the interior, following the trail of her attackers, but she didn't know that.

In the hospital a week later Diane and Peter were married. It wasn't the wedding they'd imagined.

A month after that, Diane realized she was pregnant.

10

It was raining lightly when Junko and Hideko walked out of the lobby of the Kyoto Royal Hotel. Hideko opened her umbrella and held it high to cover them both. 'I need a longer arm!' she chimed.

'I'll hold it if you want,' Junko said, taking the bright thing from Hideko's hand. It was covered with Mickey Mouses. 'Where are we going?'

'We'll go to Sanjusangendo Temple first, where we'll see the thousand and one statues of Kannon, and the thousand-armed great Kannon overlooking them all.' She looked up at Junko. 'OK?'

'Great.' Junko found herself returning the little bow that accompanied much of Hideko's speech. *Oh my God, I'm turning Japanese*, she thought, but she liked it, the courtesy of it. It also served to keep a distance between them, which suited Junko just fine. 'Enryo', she had read: 'the Japanese custom of holding back'. There was a certain grace in it.

They got on a bus and headed south. Junko unfolded the map she'd picked up at the hotel. Each temple was marked with a reverse swastika, which was weird, but had been the case for ever, according to Hideko. 'The Nazis were very bad to steal this sign,' she said, 'and turn it around for their own purpose.'

The Nazis were very bad, period, Junko thought, but Japan was allied to them in World War II. Her parents had spoken a little about Okinawa, and the occupation of Japan, but she realized she didn't know much detail about the war at all.

Sanjusangendo was amazing. They walked slowly along the corridor before the thousand and one Boddisatva Kannons in a crowd of visitors who all seemed stunned by the sight. There was absolute silence until they neared the table where a monk was stamping the temple's name and logo on pieces of paper as souvenirs. The gentle *thwap thwap* was like a call to worship. Junko had never gone to church as a child. She'd had no experience of religious feeling, or connection to anything much at all outside herself and her family. But here, in a strange hall in a strange country, she found herself suddenly and inexplicably wanting to weep. This feeling was compounded when Hideko handed her a small leather-bound book. 'For collecting,' she said. 'For you.' Junko noticed that other

51

people had similar books they were holding out for the monk to stamp.

'*Arigato*,' she managed to mumble as she took the book from Hideko's hand.

'*Do itashi-mashite*,' Hideko replied, putting her arm through Junko's. 'My pleasure, ma'am.' And she silvered the air with her laugh.

★   ★   ★

They went to the Okutan tofu restaurant for lunch, a delightful place hidden in the trees near Kiyomizu Temple in eastern Kyoto. They ate *goma dofu* and *yamaimo* and tempura tofu, with wasabi, sweet potato, sesame seeds, soy sauce and lots of pickled everything. The main dish was tofu hot-pot, blocks of tofu dipped in a sort of soy-sauce soup. And rice, of course. They sat on cushions on a tatami mat on the floor. They drank green tea until they couldn't drink another drop.

'How long is your holiday?' Hideko asked.

'I think I told you, I'm not sure yet. What's happened, you see . . . my parents died about three months ago.'

'Ah! Both? Was it an accident?'

Junko laughed. 'My parents didn't *do* accidents. No, it just happened. Natural causes . . . '

'I'm very sorry, Junko. You must be very sad.'

'It took some time to clear out . . . to sell the house and stuff. But when I'd done it, I thought, *I'll go to Japan*. Take some time out.'

'Why Japan?'

'My mom and dad met here. It was during the war.' Junko looked down at her potter's hands. This was the first time in years that there were no traces of paint or glaze or clay under her fingernails.

'Ah, so. You came here,' Hideko tilted her head, 'to be near them?'

'Well, I guess I did, but now I'm thinking it's not possible, what I wanted. Anyway,' she waved her hand as if brushing away a wasp, 'I needed a vacation. So here I am.'

They paid their bill and went walking down the steep street towards town. The shops were bursting with goods of all sizes and shapes, kimonos, sweets, umbrellas, fans, paper lanterns, toys, all brightly coloured and gaudily displayed. It was like walking through Aladdin's cave.

'Tomorrow, will you come to my home? Meet my parents? Eat with us?'

Junko nodded. 'I'd love to.' She was, after all, free to do as she pleased, especially now that she wasn't tethered to a hopeless quest that would surely only have ended in tears.

11

Diane had stopped smiling. It was as if the musculature required had ceased to function. Peter was desperate to do something to help, but could think of nothing. After the wedding, they had moved into married quarters: one half of a Quonset hut, consisting of two rooms. It had been agreed that Diane would give the baby up for adoption; after the rape, sexual intercourse had been impossible for a month or more, and all concerned assumed that the child was a product of the rape. Only Peter and Diane knew that the child could be theirs. Or not.

Diane would give birth when the time came, and the baby would fly from her womb into the world without passing into Diane's view. She sat out the time like a Death Row inmate, rarely going out of their rooms except to the outhouse, which need became more frequent as the months went by, so she got a bowl from the mess to use as a chamber pot. This was especially useful during the night; there were rats and spiders everywhere, along with deadly pit vipers.

She spent her time reading whatever she

could lay her hands on, which ranged from the Shakespeare she'd brought with her from home to the *History of Japan* Peter found in his office. Tokyo was in flames. Bombs had been dropped. The war was over, and the occupation begun. She was vaguely aware of all this. But her own personal horror overwhelmed everything else.

At night, she gradually succumbed to Peter's attempts to hold her. But she wouldn't let him touch her belly, and she avoided touching it herself. She wanted to detach herself, to be simply an observer of this process of growth. When the child started moving Diane thought she'd go mad.

They put her right out for the birth. But she came around more quickly than anyone expected. A young Red Cross nurse from Boston found Diane gazing intently at the cot where her baby lay, out of sight. 'Can I see it?' Diane whispered.

'Him,' Nurse Hawkins said. 'It's a boy.' She saw Diane flinch and realized her mistake. 'Best not, I think, under the circumstances.' She stood between Diane and the child. 'I'm taking him away now.'

Unbearable, Diane thought with a hole in her gut so large and hungry it might consume her. *This can't happen.* She struggled up in her bed and reached towards the cot. 'Please,' she pleaded, 'just let me see him.'

Nurse Hawkins turned her back to Diane and prepared to lift the baby up.

'OK,' Diane said, grabbing a notebook and pen from the table beside her bed. She scribbled her name and address on a page and tore it out. 'But will you give this to whoever . . . ' She stumbled here. 'Can I at least know how he is?'

'It's not usual.' The nurse softened for a moment and took the paper from Diane's hand. 'I can't promise anything.'

'Thank you.' Diane's voice was barely audible. She slumped back on to the pillow and wept.

Peter found her asleep when he came, her face blotchy and tear-stained, her tiny body back to something like its original shape. Her fine blond hair was stuck like gauze to her forehead. The vice that had been clamped hard round his heart for so long let up some; at least this much was over. They were cleaned out of one part of the problem. They could start again.

He thought of his brothers, Glen and Gordy. Each had three children, born with no hiccups as far as Peter was aware. Or maybe people didn't discuss those kinds of hiccups. The doctor had told Peter that their baby wasn't quite right. All for the best, then, Peter thought. But he couldn't bring himself to tell Diane. Not yet, anyway. They needed to put the baby behind them for now, and maybe for ever.

He reached out and brushed his wife's hair from her face. 'Sweetheart,' he whispered, 'hello.' He sat down on the edge of the bed.

Diane opened her eyes, but shut them again immediately. 'I saw him,' she said. 'Not his face, but his shape.' She struggled to open her eyes again. 'Is he ours? Oh, Pete, what have we done?'

He took her hand in his and lied. 'No. He wasn't ours. He's gone now.' Peter didn't want to know. 'The important thing is to rest, and get better, and think of our future.'

Diane hugged her hollow belly. 'Gone,' she said; 'oh my God in heaven, he's gone.'

'Shhhh . . . '

Suddenly the wail that had been waiting for nine months to emerge escaped. Diane roared till the windows rattled. Two nurses came running up to quieten her. 'Mrs Bayliss, that's enough now. You'll upset the others,' Nurse Hawkins snapped. Diane curled up into a ball under the sheets.

'Leave me alone,' she sobbed through the bedding.

Peter nodded an apology to the room and turned back to Diane. He leaned over and whispered urgently, 'It's going to be OK, honey. You'll see. I've got orders to go to Washington. We'll do a year there and then I'll get out and we'll move to Houston and be near your folks and all this will be over and done with, like it never happened at all. You'll see, but, Diane, you've got to *try*, really try. Come on, sweetheart, we can do this together. I need your help here. Diane?'

There was no response.

12

Junko was getting good at Kyoto buses. She'd been riding around all day, just to get a feel for the place. Travellers jammed themselves on and off at every stop, laden with shopping, children, briefcases and strollers. Kyoto was a busy city, and if the people weren't exactly gregarious, they were polite. Most managed to avoid staring at Junko for too long; they had to look up to do so, after all. Later, she got a 204 to Hideko's house, which was near Kinkakuji Temple. It was early evening when she stepped off the bus to find Hideko waiting for her.

They walked five minutes to the house, which stood on its own but in a tight cluster of other dwellings and shops. It was modern in appearance, but upon entering Junko found herself in a traditional Japanese home, with sliding paper screens and tatami mats on the floor. Junko removed her shoes at the door and was given an embarrassingly tiny pair of soft slippers to wear. Her big feet hung well over the ends. 'I think you are very firmly attached to the ground, Junko!' Hideko's laugh was like silver coins dropping from the sky.

They went into the formal living room, where Mr and Mrs Tanaka were waiting.

'*Konichiwa*, Junko.' Fujio Tanaka bowed, beaming. 'Welcome to our home.'

'*Konichiwa*,' Yuki Tanaka echoed. The couple could almost be taken for twins. Both were Hideko's height, greying at the temples, with the same crinkly bright eyes.

'Hello,' Junko replied. 'Thank you.' She felt like a large oyster washed up on a beach of pearls. Or a scraggy rhododendron in a garden of roses. She couldn't wait to sit down.

'I can see why Hideko wants to paint you. You are very beautiful,' Yuki said.

'Very bountiful!' Junko answered. 'There's a lot of me!'

'Ah, so,' Fujio nodded. 'This is very good for Hideko.'

They settled around the table and Yuki brought out the makings for dinner: a bowl of dough, a bowl of octopus sliced into small pieces, several plates of pickles including ginger, plums and bite-size vegetables. There was soya and Bulldog sauce, and a pot of mayonnaise. The rice balls were wrapped round with thin sheets of seaweed.

She plugged in an electric grill with small

round scoops in it and set about making *takoyaki*, which turned out to be pancake balls with a piece of octopus in the middle of each. They were eaten with a squirt of fruity Bulldog and a dollop of mayonnaise.

Junko was trying to get the hang of chopsticks. She was already developing a love of authentic Japanese food, which was far different from anything her parents had given her, and wanted to eat it right. But after the third *takoyaki* ended up in her lap, Yuki insisted on giving her a fork.

'Keep trying,' Fujio smiled, 'and you will succeed. But now, you can eat!' Yuki poured green tea, nodding her agreement.

'I'm so sorry to hear about the death of your parents,' Fujio said.

'Thanks. That's very sweet of you. But . . .' Junko stopped, and wiped the corners of her mouth with a napkin.

'Yes?' he asked.

'I feel like I hardly knew them, really. I mean, we weren't close. So I guess that makes it easier.'

'Or, possibly, harder?' Yuki said.

Junko felt confused by this remark. She'd nearly convinced herself that she was only lightly touched by grief now. 'I'm not sure what you mean,' she said, stabbing another *takoyaki* with her fork.

'Perhaps your sense of loss is compounded, because it is a reflection of a loss you've always felt?' Yuki tilted her head in Junko's direction.

'Maybe.' Junko felt her scalp prickling. She wriggled on her cushion. 'I don't know.' She looked at Yuki, feeling desperate to change the subject. 'Do you work? Besides — ' Junko swept her arm towards the kitchen — 'in the house?'

'*Hai*. I work for the town hall. Local government.'

'What part of Houston do you live in?' Fujio asked. 'I stay at the Hyatt when I'm there.'

Junko smiled. 'I'm not far from there. Montrose.'

'Of course! The artists' community.'

Yuki offered another *takoyaki* but Junko shook her head. 'I'm stuffed! It was delicious. Thank you.'

'And where did your parents live?'

'Clear Lake City.' Junko didn't want to talk about her parents.

'Ah, so! NASA. Did your father work for NASA? The 'race into space'?'

Hideko noticed Junko's discomfort and jumped up. 'Come with me, Junko. I'll show you where I paint.' She shook her head at her parents. 'My mother and father are philosophers. I am an artist!'

Junko stood gratefully, and Hideko took her hand and led her away.

They went to a large room at the back of the house. The floor was tiled, and the wooden walls were stacked with canvases. One half-finished still-life stood on an easel in the middle of the room. It was of a cutting board spread with dead fish and other seafood. Junko recognized the squid and the shrimp but nothing else. The detail was astonishing, the glistening scales and bulging eyes. Hideko had talent, that was very clear.

'Do you think you could stand for me?' Hideko asked. 'I'd like to paint your whole form, not just the face. Is that OK, ma'am?' she giggled.

Junko nodded.

'Not tomorrow. My teacher comes then. Thursday?'

'I don't see why not.' Junko smiled at Hideko. 'You're not going to make me into a monster or anything, are you?'

'Impossible! Anyway, I am not Picasso. I am Hideko! I paint things as I see them.'

Junko was looking through the pictures stacked against the walls. She came across one of Eikando Temple in the autumn, with the Japanese maples blazing red.

'*Kouyo*,' Hideko said as she came to stand

beside Junko. 'That's what we call the autumn leaves.'

'Kouyo,' Junko repeated. 'Beautiful.'

'If you stay until November, you can see it with your own eyes.'

Who knows? Junko thought. I don't know anything.

'So. Is 9 a.m. OK on Thursday? I like best the morning light in here.'

'Fine. I guess I'll get going now. I want to write some letters.'

She said her goodbyes to the Tanakas, and caught the bus back to her hotel. She wanted to tell Gloria about her decision not to contact Hiromi Mitsuki. She needed to explain, mainly to herself.

13

Diane left the hospital after a week. She'd hardly eaten and was back to her normal size. Her breasts were still swollen, but the doctor had given her something to dry up the milk. That had hurt, the engorgement and leaking. She could hear her baby crying like a constant low hum in her head, wanting sustenance that she couldn't give him. *Him.* Her little boy.

A month later they were off to Washington DC. They found a house in Alexandria, Virginia, and Peter commuted to the Pentagon every day. Diane stayed at home, walking along the Potomac in the mornings and spending the afternoons in the library reading up on Japan. The day before they'd left Okinawa, she'd received a note from Nurse Hawkins, whose conscience had been pricking her:

Dear Mrs Bayliss,

I hear you and your husband are leaving here. I wanted to let you know that your son went to Kyoto — not through the normal channels, it was arranged by a man here who thought it best that the child be brought up in a spiritual environment. I can't tell you his name because I don't know it. All I know is the name of a woman in Kyoto who has something to do with it. She is Hiromi Mitsuki. The only address I have is Eikando Temple.

I thought it would be useless to pass on your address to her. It is unlikely that she speaks English.

I'm so sorry for your sadness.
Yours,
Dolores Hawkins

Diane had shown Peter the letter. She'd wanted to go to Kyoto on the way home, but it had been impossible. They were travelling home on a converted navy hospital ship and would be nineteen days at sea. Peter had wanted nothing to do with the child in any case.

'We need to leave this behind us, Diane. For the sake of our own children.' They were sitting at the dining table in their tiny living room.

'My blood has fallen here! You don't understand that! I just — '

'It's futile!'

'It isn't — '

'Yes it is! In this case, it is.'

Diane had turned from him. 'Can't you see, Pete? It won't go away.'

'Wrong!' Peter was angry now. 'You couldn't be more wrong! You can decide, Diane.' He banged his fist on the table. 'Do you think this is easy for me? Well?'

Diane was shocked. She'd depended utterly on her husband, but hadn't considered his feelings at all. She'd been too rocked by her own. 'Oh, my dear. I'm so sorry.' She stood up and put her arms around him and held on tight.

'Listen,' Peter mumbled into her hair, 'we'll get out of here and be able to see things more clearly. OK?'

'Uh-huh,' Diane had replied, thinking, *OK. Not now. But definitely later. No matter how long it takes.*

★ ★ ★

So they had sailed away. And now Diane was making Japan her business. She learned about the archipelago that stretches some 1,860 miles, from eastern Siberia down almost to Taiwan, a narrow chain consisting of thousands of islands, 75 per cent of it mountainous, forested, sometimes volcanic.

She learned that Japan only emerged from strictly enforced, self-imposed isolation in the

1860s, and when it did, the country threw itself headlong into modernization while retaining its emperor and its cultural traditions. She studied Hokusai's Views of Mount Fuji. She read Lafcadio Hearn and Basho. She was particularly interested in Kyoto, a city with more than 1,800 Buddhist temples and hundreds of Shinto shrines.

Shinto (the Way of the Gods) is the old religion. It involves worship of *kami*, or the gods that exist in all things. Because people become *kami* when they die, ancestors are revered.

Buddhism was imported from India via China and Korea. It teaches that enlightenment can be gained through meditation, the elimination of desire and awareness of the transience of life. There is no god, there is only the constant straining towards a higher consciousness, and the search for wisdom and compassion. Diane was shocked. She kept notes.

Peter was hoping for a new pregnancy to erase the memory of the first one. But there was scar tissue where her vagina was torn in the attack, and then torn again during the birth, so intercourse was still uncomfortable for Diane. They slipped into a pattern of infrequent sex, a pattern that stuck.

Peter got out of the service in 1947. They

moved to Houston and he set up his business as planned. Diane had never told her parents or her sister about the rape or the child. She couldn't bear to do it now either, though all had noticed the change in her. Her old vibrancy had dulled into an intense melancholy. It was heartbreaking to see. *It must be the war*, her parents thought. Helen sensed something deeper, but couldn't persuade Diane to talk about it.

Helen had met Deke during her last year of high school. She was planning to go on and study art, but Deke had blown through town and captured her heart completely. He was fifty-eight years old; she was eighteen. But the widower Deacon Ellis had so much charm, and so much love for Helen, that nobody seemed to notice the age difference. He was a wealthy man, in the oil business, and would look after her for the nine years of their happy marriage, and all the years after his death as well.

And so, the first five years rolled in and out like Gulf tides. Peter's business kept expanding until he finally had his own office building downtown. He learned to play golf. Diane took watercolour classes, read novels, sewed and knitted and kept an immaculate house. She saw Helen and Molly weekly for iced tea and small talk. It was a gentle routine, almost satisfactory. *Almost.*

One Saturday morning Diane suggested to Peter that they drive to Galveston for lunch. It was only an hour away, and it was a cool April day, so they could stroll along the beach without fear of melting into the sand.

As they settled into their seats at the Old Galveston Hotel, Diane slid a piece of paper across the table. Peter picked it up and read. It was the note that Dolores Hawkins had sent Diane in Okinawa.

'Years, Diane. It's been how many? Seven years?'

'I know.'

'Well?' Peter sighed. 'What about it?'

'I want to go to Kyoto.'

'What?'

'Please, Pete. We can afford it.'

'But what do you expect to find, exactly? This is foolish. Ridiculous. It's asking for trouble, to bring all that up again.'

'I don't expect anything. I just think it's worth a try.'

Peter shook his head. 'This is crazy.'

'We could use a vacation.' She reached for his hand. 'Pete, it would settle things for me. Even if we don't find him. At least we'll have tried.'

Peter had never been very good at saying no to his wife.

'And they say Kyoto is a beautiful place,' she added.

'What do you want from this, Diane? A son to bring home? A half-caste son?' he asked her gently.

'No, no, no. That's not it. I just want to see him. To make sure he's OK. To make him real.'

'It was all real enough at the time,' Peter said bitterly.

'Not to me it wasn't. It's like a dream to me, a dream that won't end. I can't wake up. I need to end it. I need to see him.'

'What if he's not there?'

Diane shrugged. 'So be it.'

They flew to Japan at the beginning of May.

14

Wednesday was a day Junko would spend all by herself. She got up early and headed for eastern Kyoto. She wanted to walk along the Path of Philosophy, Tetsugakuno-michi. It ran from Ginkakuji Temple along a canal heading south to Nanzenji Temple. Eikando was on the way. Then she was going to shop. Junko had never been much of a shopper, but she was determined to get something nice for Gloria and for Billy, and a souvenir for herself also.

Ginkakuji was breathtaking, with its magical Zen gardens and pond full of brightly coloured carp. The day was gorgeous too, hot sun mediated by a cool breeze from the hills. Junko wandered through the halls, admiring the paintings of Ike Taiga, Yosa Buson, Tomioka Tessai and Okuda Gensuo. She particularly liked Yosa Buson's magical depictions of plants and flying birds; the movement created seemed to be towards another world, a world Junko knew nothing about.

She started on the path, thinking about her mother and father. Had she loved them? It hadn't been presented to her as an option, really. It was never discussed. Had she ever loved anyone? Certainly no man. She'd had lovers over the years, but they'd drifted in and out of her life like the weather: it happened, but one had little control over when or where. *That's not fair*, Junko thought. *I never invited anyone in to stay. It's me.* Why was she thinking about love, anyway? On this Path of Philosophy, on a gorgeous summer day, on the other side of the world?

Junko thought of Billy and Glory, her two closest friends. What was she to them? She wandered along the sparkling water of the canal in the quiet of the morning, picturing Billy singing out loud at his wheel, and Glory in her nurse's uniform, handing out leaflets for the women's health day she organized every year. The pictures made her smile, and just at that moment two herons flew over her head, going north together. They seemed to hang a moment in the sky above her, a hovering presence of such grace and beauty that Junko's mouth dropped open and she stopped in her tracks. They flew on, and Junko moved forward again, feeling like a child in a fairy tale: there was magic afoot.

She came to Eikando, and was drawn into its grounds. She realized she was hungry. There was a soba-noodle bar under an awning near the entrance. She ordered some lunch and when it came she sat at a table and looked at it, perplexed. Kenichiro, who'd brought it, smiled. 'I will show you.'

There was a wicker tray of buckwheat noodles and a bowl of a sort of soy-sauce soup, with bits of green onion and wasabi floating in it. He indicated that Junko should take a mouthful of noodles in her chopsticks and dip them into the soup before eating them. She should hold the bowl under her chin for best effect. Junko managed to get a good bite in, nodding at the same time.

'You like hot?' Kenichiro enquired, holding forth a little wooden pot in the shape of a roundish chilli pepper.

'I do.' Junko swallowed, and the man sprinkled the spice into her bowl.

She was getting better at chopsticks, but still ended up with dribbles on her chin and a noodle or two in her lap. It was worth it though. She was beginning to think she could live on Japanese food for ever. She wasn't missing hot dogs at all.

She left the table when she finished, thanking the man and nodding. She made her way to the same stone step she'd sat on last time she was here. Would she find Hiromi Mitsuki if she tried? This was a day full of questions. She looked up through the maple leaves at the powder-blue sky, the same sky as was over Texas, just a different slice of it.

Before leaving Eikando she went to the little gift shop and bought three postcards. The woman who served her asked where she was from. 'Texas,' Junko answered.

'Ah, so.' She tilted her head and looked Junko straight in the eye with an oddly penetrative warmth. 'Do you like Japan?'

'Very much, yes I do,' Junko said, squirming in the glow of this extraordinary woman's gaze. She backed away, and gave a little wave before finding her way back to the Path of Philosophy. *Who on earth was that?* she asked herself. She felt like she'd been in the presence of an angel.

Junko went to town. Hiromi Mitsuki closed the shop for ten minutes and went to see Toshie the potter.

'I think we have company, Toshie-chan,' she said, smiling.

15

The department store Junko chose was nine storeys high. She wandered around, fascinated by both the differences in what was displayed and the similarities: Bloomingdale's with a twist. Very stylish and up-to-the-minute clothes, shoes, accessories, luggage — anything you could want. The electrical appliances took up two floors.

Junko found a section that was all traditional Japanese designs. She bought a matching fan and silk handkerchief in a pale yellow and brown pattern for Helen, a six-foot-long embroidered scarf for Gloria, but Billy? She couldn't decide. It was all incredibly expensive, but she wasn't worried about money. She'd keep looking.

For herself, she got a padded house jacket with the face of a traditional geisha on the back and Japanese characters down the front. It was cotton, with silk trim around the edges, in navy blue and black.

She started back to the hotel with her purchases, but her attention was captured by the sound of a gong. She was near the Yasaka-jinja Shinto shrine, and there was a ceremony taking place. As she got closer she could hear drums and reedy squealing flutes.

She entered the large open yard with its gaudily coloured pavilion in the middle. There were children everywhere, dressed in kimonos and wooden sandals and being tidied up by their parents. There were lots of infants, too. About thirty men were sitting under a canopy playing various sizes of flute, from enormous to piccoloesque. The drummers were mostly standing behind them. The gong was on the pavilion, and being struck regularly. It was a cheerful celebration, everyone looking like they were about to burst into song or the giggles. Junko stood listening for a while, feeling lifted by the occasion, although it was nothing to do with her at all.

She stopped at a huge bookshop on the way home and got a small volume in English about the two religions, Shinto and Buddhism, which coexist quite happily in Japanese society. Most Japanese would say they belong to both. She learned that what she'd witnessed was possibly a *miyamairi*, the Shinto version of baptism, which happens a month after the child is born.

Amaterasu, the sun-goddess, is the principal deity in Shinto. She was once upon a time so offended by the misdeeds of her brother that she came to Earth and hid in a cave. The world became a pitch-dark and evil place. Other gods and goddesses gathered around the cave to try and figure out a way to get her to come out. They held a prehistoric rave, and one goddess danced so wildly that her clothes whirled right off her body and the others cheered. Amaterasu was curious, and peeked out to see what was going on. 'We're celebrating a new goddess,' they told her. When she came out to have a look, a mirror was held up and she saw herself. She agreed never to hide again.

I've been hiding in a cave all my life, Junko thought, *and in a huff, too*. She put the book away and took a shower before going to the dining room for some dinner. As she stood under the powerful spray she was reminded of her parents' house. She remembered one morning when she was very small walking into their bathroom and finding them in the shower together. Her father was slowly, lovingly soaping Diane's back. They didn't see her. As she turned and walked away she heard the Buddha's humming for the first time, and it soothed her.

The dining room was crowded as usual. Junko ended up sharing a table with a businesswoman from Chiba, near Tokyo. She was a buyer for Sogo, a huge department store there, and was in Kyoto to buy kimonos. Her name was Chie Yamamoto. She was just Junko's age, thirty-six, and they soon discovered they shared a birthday, 3 August.

'How funny!' Chie exclaimed. 'Maybe we are sisters!'

Junko laughed. The idea of a sister was quite beyond her imagining. 'Do you live alone?' There was no wedding ring, but Junko wasn't sure of the Japanese tradition in that regard.

'No.' Chie shook her head. 'I live with my husband.' Chie was possibly the most elegant woman Junko had ever seen. She was wearing a beautifully tailored sleeveless linen dress in a pale peachy colour. Its matching jacket was hanging on the back of Chie's chair. Her hair was cut very short, and her pale porcelain skin glowed.

'Kids?' Junko asked, more nosy than she'd ever be at home.

'My husband is my only child!' Chie exclaimed with a wave of her hand. 'I don't think I could manage another one.' She frowned. 'I need to decide soon, actually. I have one niece, who is beautiful. I don't know.' She shrugged, shaking her head. 'What about you?'

Junko felt herself blushing. 'No. I mean, I'm not involved with anyone right now.'

'Ah,' Chie said. 'Are you lonely?'

'Not till now. I never thought I was lonely before. Just alone.'

'And now?'

How was Junko managing to get herself into these conversations with total strangers? Conversations that hit her in the heart? *On the road,* she thought. *It's the traveller's curse, to be so intensely in the world that you're reminded daily of your separateness from it.* 'I'm fine,' she answered with a sigh. 'I've never been here before, is all.'

They finished their meal, feeling like old friends. They decided to go for a walk along the Kamo-gawa River. It was a hot and humid night, and people were out in droves, hoping to catch a breeze at the water's edge. The moon was full and round and hung above the river like a magic lantern. They sat down on a bench.

'Years ago, people rinsed their long bolts of newly dyed silk in the Kamo-gawa. The river flowed like a rippling rainbow!'

'Really?'

'*Hai.*'

'It must have been beautiful.'

Chie nodded. 'Many poets wrote about it.'

'So many people!' Junko said, watching the crowd flow past with the river.

'Moon-viewing. A favourite Japanese pastime. *Tsuki-mi*, the main moon-viewing festival, is in the autumn. The harvest moon.'

'*Tsuki-mi*,' Junko repeated, gazing out over the water, which sparkled in the moonglow. She felt she could sit there all night. But Chie stood.

'I'm catching an early train,' she yawned. Junko rose with her and they started towards the hotel.

'Everybody's so nice here,' Junko said.

Chie laughed. 'We are a very deferential people. But the hierarchies in Japan are deadly.'

'What?'

'You have to know exactly how low to bow to your superiors.'

Junko looked puzzled.

'It's complicated. Don't worry' — she took Junko's arm — 'you don't have to bow to anyone.'

'Is it work you're talking about?' Junko wanted to know.

'Not just work. Life.'

16

In the spring of 1953, Diane and Peter Bayliss arrived in Kyoto. They found a hotel downtown and made themselves ready. They went to Eikando Temple and asked for Hiromi Mitsuki. She took them to Yuji, who was seven then.

As Diane was removing her shoes on the porch of Toshie's house, trembling in her fingers and in her soul, the boy slid the screen door open and stepped into the light. '*Oka-san*,' he said, and then, 'Mother,' in English. He offered her his hand and led her inside. Peter followed. Toshie was preparing green tea. She gave a bow and indicated that they should sit on the floor at the low table in the middle of the room. Yuji sat between them, smiling enormously, saying nothing. Diane and Peter stared at the boy unabashedly. It was impossible to tell if he was theirs or not. His skin was a beautiful golden brown from the sun, and he had dark eyes and hair and ruddy cheeks. He wore a dark blue robe made of rough cotton cloth and tied with a sash. He had Peter's colouring, but not his Roman nose or his biggish ears. And his clothing, his manner, his surroundings made him look Japanese.

Toshie brought the tea to the table and filled beautiful ceramic cups for each of them. She said, 'The boy is very happy here.'

Diane rushed to reply, shaking her head. 'We don't want to take him away. That's not it.' She looked to Peter for help. He cleared his throat.

'The boy belongs here. We only — '

'We needed to know where he was.' There were tears wanting to come but Diane blinked them back and swallowed. 'He's my only child,' she whispered.

Toshie nodded. 'I understand.' She turned to Yuji. 'He's a fine boy. A good boy. Everybody loves Yuji.'

They drank their tea, smiled a lot, and something inside Diane Bayliss shifted softly into place. It was love.

Peter and Diane stayed in Kyoto for two weeks. They saw Yuji and Toshie and Hiromi every day. They ate Kenichiro's soba noodles and walked the grounds of Eikando and many other temples. Yuji said very little, but spread a brightness around him wherever he went. Everyone knew him.

Diane was in heaven. She was beginning to feel forgiven. Peter's frustration with not knowing if he was Yuji's father or not was a seed, but it would grow.

Every year after that they visited Kyoto for two weeks in May, except for 1959, the year Junko was born. Diane was sick throughout the pregnancy, and furious that she couldn't go to see her son.

Bird of time
In Kyoto, pining
For Kyoto

Basho, trans. Lucien Stryk

17

Diane and Helen were walking along the beach near Kemah on the morning of 13 January 1959. Deke had been dead for eleven years, and every year on this day they walked his favourite stretch of the Gulf in his memory. Suddenly Diane grabbed Helen's arm and bent double. She was violently sick.

'Where did that come from?' Helen helped Diane to stand up and move closer to the water. She got a hanky out of her bag and dipped it in the surf, then wrung it out and dabbed Diane's forehead.

'Oh God,' Diane groaned. 'This is the third day in a row.'

Helen's eyebrows shot up. 'You know what this looks like? Huh?' Helen and Deke had decided not to try for children — Deke had six already — but Helen knew the signs.

'Oh, God,' Diane groaned again. She sat down on the sand and started crying.

'Now, honey, it's a blessing,' Helen soothed, 'and about time too.'

'After all these years . . . ' Diane started.

'Uh-huh, that's right. You've hit the jackpot, sugar.'

'No! I don't want it!' She jumped up as if to run away but retched again, clutching her belly.

'Oh. I see.' Helen wasn't really surprised. Diane and Peter lived quite isolated lives. When Deke was alive the couples got together for bridge every Friday, but after he died, any social contact other than the occasional walk on the beach fizzled out. Their get-togethers with Molly Greengrass went the same way. 'So,' she asked quietly, 'what are you going to do?'

Diane looked at Helen with despair. 'What the hell do you think I'm going to do?'

The wind was whipping up a storm. Helen pulled her coat tighter and put her arm around her sister. 'It'll be OK.'

'It'll have to be,' Diane snapped. 'I haven't told Pete.'

They watched a low-flying flock of pelicans sail over the sea.

'That's luck! That's bird-luck, honey.' Helen squeezed Diane's shoulders. 'Tell him soon. OK?'

Diane nodded. They turned around and headed home.

★ ★ ★

When she told her husband she was pregnant, he was stunned. He hadn't the foggiest idea how to react. He'd kept his bitterness about Yuji simmering under the surface, but had outlived his desire for another child. At thirty-nine, he felt too old and too set in his ways; they both were. How would they manage?

On the other hand, no proof of paternity would be required this time. Confirmation of his virility was at hand. He should be delighted.

'How do you feel?' he asked his wife.

'In shock,' she answered. They were sitting at their kitchen table. 'Sick.'

'It's not that awful, Diane,' Peter started, but she stopped him.

'I mean nausea,' she spoke wearily. 'I was never sick with Yuji.'

'You're older. Maybe that's — '

'You're older too!'

'Yes.' He took her hand in his. 'It'll be OK.'

'That's just what I've been hearing all my life! And finally, when it's finally really OK, THIS!' she howled.

Peter didn't know what to say. He had about seven months to try and figure it out, but he never did.

The gestation seemed as slow as the world. Diane was sick every day of it, right up until the last week, when the puking stopped and the little practice contractions began. The delivery was smooth, ten hours exactly. When the doctor handed her infant daughter to Diane, she found she couldn't even look at the child, and was relieved when the baby was wheeled away for the night.

Peter was somewhat happier; a daughter would be nice enough, but he'd have preferred a boy, his own boy.

18

Junko was due at Hideko's at 9 a.m., but she got up at six to have breakfast with Chie before she had to go. Over *mirinboshi* and green tea, Chie told her about Bodhidharma, who was a Buddhist missionary from India. He's thought of as the father of martial arts. Because of his long travels on dangerous roads, and his non-violent attitudes, he developed the throws, pins and chops that eventually turned into kung-fu. He was also so highly spiritual that he cut his eyelids off so that he could be 'eternally vigilant'. Bodhidharma brought Buddhism to China in the fifth century AD, from where it made its way to Korea and then Japan.

On finishing her story, Chie presented Junko with a small brightly painted papier-mâché head of Doruma, the Japanese name for Bodhidharma. It was mainly red, with gold, black and white designs. The eyes were blank.

'This is for wishing. When you make your wish, you colour one eye in. When your wish comes true, you colour in the other eye. OK?'

'*Arigato*, Chie. It's very sweet of you.

Thanks a lot.' Junko was positively awash with presents. It was excruciating. Was she supposed to give something back? What, then?

Chie gathered her things. 'I'll be back in two weeks. Will you be here?'

'Not sure yet. Maybe.' Junko took a last sip of tea and scribbled her address in Houston on a piece of paper. 'Come and see me some time? There's a lot to buy in Texas. Wait a minute.' Junko got the camera out of her bag and aimed it carefully at the grinning Chie. Photography made her nervous; it was so real. She pressed the button.

Chie gave a quick bow. 'Thank you for the invitation. I've always wanted to ride a horse.' She waved as she left the dining room.

With time to kill, Junko went to her room to write to her Aunt Helen. She took one of the postcards of Eikando she'd bought the day before. It was definitely her favourite of the temples she'd seen.

Dear Helen,
Kyoto's glorious!
Why don't you come out and join me? I think I might stay for a while, maybe a month or two. Think about it!
Lots of love,
June x

She hopped on a bus and headed for Hideko's. Yuki opened the door just as she was about to knock. Junko looked down at her, startled. Hideko looked so much like her mother, with her curly black hair, pale face and warm smile. Yuki wasn't as slim any more, but Junko imagined she had been once.

'Come in, Junko.' Yuki stood aside. Junko entered the house and took her shoes off. She noticed that there was a new pair of lime-green mules lined up with the others, just her size. Yuki pushed them towards Junko with a twinkle in her eye. 'For you.'

'*Dohmo arigato.*' Junko bowed. She didn't know which was more embarrassing, her big feet in tiny slippers or the fact that Yuki had had to get Junko some that fitted. '*Dohmo,*' she repeated as she slid into them. Her phrase-book was coming in very handy.

Yuki led Junko to Hideko's room. There was a radiance there that was truly breathtaking, with the sun shining in through the open slats of the blinds, striping the floor. Hideko was squirting paint on to her palette. Junko noticed there was a lot of white.

'Good morning.' She dipped her head in Hideko's direction and sat down on a wooden chair in the middle of the room.

'*Konichiwa*, friend,' Hideko said. 'Are you ready?' She waved her brush in the air.

'Sure am,' Junko answered. 'Just tell me where to stand.'

'By the window, I think.' Hideko pointed to the back wall of the studio, where the sun was streaming in. 'In the brightest light.'

Junko walked over and gazed out into the garden. There was a pond, and just as she looked out a frog leaped from a rock into the water, making a splash. She thought of the poem by Basho she'd read in her parents' house: *Breaking the silence/of an ancient pond/a frog jumped into water — /a deep resonance.* Junko was suddenly overcome with grief. She knew she would never stop missing her mother and father. It would be a life-long preoccupation. She wondered how she would survive it.

Hideko was watching her, although Junko didn't realize it. The young woman had sensed from the beginning a deep sadness in Junko. She wanted to capture it on canvas, and this looked like the perfect moment. 'Shall I start?' she asked lightly.

'OK.' Junko kept her eyes on the pond and Hideko set to work. Junko was self-conscious at first, but fairly soon lost herself in the ripples on the water. She'd always been good at being still. Hideko painted for two hours without stopping then declared herself finished for the day. They went into the living room for an early lunch with Yuki. She had prepared miso soup, and was making rice balls. 'Can I help?' Junko asked.

'Here.' Yuki handed her a square sheet of seaweed and a dollop of rice. She showed Junko how to shape the rice, holding it in the palm of her hand, and then wrap the seaweed around it. Junko's efforts were clumsy and her rice balls misshapen, but both Hideko and Yuki applauded as she put the last one on the plate. Her cheeks pinked, but she was delighted.

Hideko walked Junko to the bus stop when they were finished. 'I will call you when it's ready, maybe in one week?' She looked for Junko's response. 'You'll still be here?'

'Yep. I will.'

'Good.' The women hugged each other. *This could get to be a habit*, Junko thought, *hugging*. She got on the bus and waved goodbye.

Junko spent the rest of the afternoon walking along the river, trying to decide what to wish for with her Doruma. True love? Happiness? A cruise down the Nile? A hot dog? What she wanted most in the world was for her mother to look at her, just look, and see someone there. But that was never going to happen.

Before she climbed into bed that night, she drew one eye on Doruma's face. Her wish was simply to *get over it*. To move on. She screwed her eyes tight and wished hard.

19

Yuji makes his way to his spot up the hillside. He is lean and wiry like a mountain goat, with a wide moon-face and steel-wool eyebrows that curl in all directions. His face is free of wrinkles and he looks nothing like his fifty years. When he arrives at the little shrine he sits and begins his prayers. It is early morning and the crickets are creaking away in the dewy grass. Yuji can make them jump into his hand by whistling.

Yuji is sitting in the lotus position. He begins his *nembutsu*. He recites the name of Amida Buddha until the Mind of Faith manifests itself. *Namu Amida Butsu. Namu Amida Butsu.* His spirit rises into the air.

★ ★ ★

On Friday morning Junko is up very early and walking the Path of Philosophy. As she approaches Eikando she notices a glow on the hillside. The closer she gets, the more astounded she becomes. It's a person! A person, sitting down, and floating in the air! Junko feels an exhilaration she can't explain.

A warm breeze blows over the canal and seems to caress her hair. She could swear she hears the Buddha's humming. She's not walking any more, she's basking in the warmth of this odd Kyoto second sun. Her skin tingles. Her eyes close. When she opens them, he's gone.

20

Molly Greengrass was getting out of her Chrysler with a bag of groceries when the thought occurred to her to call Diane and Helen. It had been a while, and June's birthday was the day after tomorrow. Molly sent the child a card every year, but hadn't seen her for some time. She'd be thirteen, a teenager, like all of Molly's three boys. They were fourteen, fifteen and seventeen, Randy, Tote and Bean.

Molly and Mort had moved from Pearland to Clear Lake ten years ago. It hadn't been easy being a Jew in Pearland, Texas. Mort had liked the idea of a small town to commute from, thought the kids would get more out of it, but what they'd got hadn't always been so pleasant. Decidedly not. There were plenty of Klan around there.

Clear Lake was a different story. There were people from all over the place, working at NASA or stationed at Ellington Field. And Diane and Helen were close by. Not that it was making much difference these days. Since June's birth, they only got together once or twice a year. *Maybe*, Molly thought, *I could put on a little party for Junie.*

She put her food away and went to the phone.

'Hello?' Diane's soft voice answered.

'Diane, it's Molly.'

'Hi there. How are you?'

'Fine, hon, just fine. I was wondering, what are you doing for Junie's birthday? I thought I'd like to see her. Haven't seen y'all since Christmas.'

'Oh, we don't do much. Just the usual.'

'Uh-huh. Well, what about coming over here? I could bake a cake. You guys eat cake, don't you?' Molly ran her free hand through her frizzy black mane. The sultry heat of south-east Texas thwarted any styling efforts she might attempt.

'Not normally, no.'

'No cake? At a birthday party?'

Diane was silent. Molly wasn't all that surprised. She'd assumed that the Bayliss family kept birthday celebrations to a minimum, having never been invited to join in. But she hadn't known they didn't mark the occasion at all. Her friend seemed stranger every year.

'Remember when we were little, up in Athens? We'd get so excited when our birthday was coming up we didn't sleep for a week before.' She paused. 'Remember,

99

Diane? When you were thirteen?'

'I do.' Diane was holding her breath. She let it go in a sigh. 'That was years ago, when Mom and Dad were alive.'

'You're the mother now.'

'I know.' Diane's voice was sharper now. 'We do things our way, that's all. Thank you, Molly, I appreciate it, but we do things our way now.'

Molly was perturbed. She held the phone scrunched between her cheek and shoulder while she poured herself a glass of tea. 'Well then, what say you and Helen and I go beach-walking one afternoon? Junie could come — '

'June has her own friends to play with,' Diane cut in. 'I'm trying to finish a quilt right now, for a charity auction,' she lied. 'I'll call you when I'm done with that. OK?'

'OK,' Molly answered, 'Call me. Diane?'

'Yes?'

'I just miss you, is all.'

Diane's heart softened some. 'I'm right around the corner practically. Just a little busy right now.'

'Oh, all right, hon. I'll talk to you later.'

Molly placed the phone in its cradle and put her hands on her plump hips, shaking her head. Molly had always been the butterball to Diane's Tinkerbell, the dark moon to Diane's fair sunshine. That sunshine was getting dimmer by the year, and Molly didn't have a clue why. But it broke her heart. And Diane's peculiar attitude towards her only child was unsettling. This, from a loving and playful childhood companion who'd liked nothing better than a get-together or a sing-along.

Diane went back to her quilting. She was making a nine-square double, scarlet and green mainly, the autumn colours of Eikando. She wanted to get it in the mail by Friday.

21

Junko was eating soba noodles at Kenichiro's stall when Hiromi approached her and sat down. 'My husband,' she said, pointing at Kenichiro. 'Good?' She pointed at the food this time.

'I love them,' Junko replied. 'I love this green stuff. Blows your head off!' She dipped her chopsticks into the dab of paste.

'Wasabi,' Hiromi said. 'I like it too.'

Junko picked up some noodles and dunked them in the soba sauce, then put them in her mouth. She was thinking about the first time she saw Hiromi and how startling it was.

'Hey,' she said when she'd chewed and swallowed. 'I saw the funniest thing this morning.'

Hiromi waited.

'It looked like — ' Junko stopped. The woman would think she was mad.

'Please go on.'

'Well, it looked like a man suspended in the air over the trees.' She laughed, embarrassed. 'Maybe I was seeing things.'

Hiromi smiled. 'And maybe not.'

Junko stared at Hiromi in wonder. Was

everyone around here touched in some way?

'Junko,' Hiromi started, and Junko nearly fell from her seat.

'How did you know my name?'

'Junko, I want to tell you a story.'

'Huh?'

Hiromi leaned in close. 'At the end of the war things were difficult for the Japanese. We were occupied. We had to learn how to be democratic. Many were maimed and crippled, physically and psychologically.'

Junko's ears pricked at this. She nodded, urging Hiromi to go on.

'Atrocities were committed. Japan still won't admit to its crimes. That would be implicating the Emperor, which is impossible.'

'Why?'

'Our emperor is God to us. Descended from God. He can't be questioned or accused.'

'I don't get it.'

Hiromi waved her hand. 'Never mind about that. Anyway, the Japanese weren't the only ones to commit war crimes.'

'No?'

'Many soldiers in wartime do heroic things, but some are not so heroic.' She looked into Junko's eyes. 'I am Hiromi Mitsuki.' Junko was speechless. She put her bowl, which she had been clutching to her, on the table. She gripped its edges and held on tight, as if expecting to be yanked from her seat. 'I want you to meet someone. Will you follow me?'

Somehow Junko managed to stumble along behind Hiromi up the winding path to Toshie's house. When they got there, Yuji was waiting in the doorway, and Junko recognized the glow she'd seen in the sky.

'*Imouto*,' he said, and took her hand in his.

Junko thought he was a monk. Yuji had the aura of Buddha himself, and if he could fly, well, that was something. She never in her wildest dreams thought she'd meet a flying monk.

Toshie loomed behind him. She was a broad woman, tall and sturdy. She was of the Ainu people, and her light skin and wavy grey hair were testaments to this fact. She looked like she was shooing Junko off, flapping her hands excitedly. Junko looked at Hiromi, not knowing what to do. Hiromi laughed. 'She wants you to come in. That's what we do in Japan when we want to say come here. You would do the opposite.' Hiromi made a beckoning gesture. 'Yes?'

Junko nodded, bewildered, and entered the house, followed by Yuji and Hiromi. Tea things were on the table. They sat on cushions and Toshie poured.

'We've been expecting you,' Hiromi said, 'ever since I called for Diane and you answered.' Junko drank her *cha* in silence. Each word struck her like a little slap. How could she know more about Junko than Junko knew herself? 'Your parents came here every year. I expect you knew that?'

'I only knew Japan. They went to Japan. That's all.'

Hiromi sighed.

'Did you know them from the war?' Junko asked.

'No. It was after the war when I met Diane and Peter. When Yuji was seven.'

Junko looked at Yuji, whose face was radiant. '*Imouto*,' he said again, and a flood of heat hit her heart. She felt like crying but didn't know why. 'You speak English,' she mumbled.

'*Hai*.' Hiromi gave a nod. 'It was necessary.'

'Were you floating in the sky this morning?' she asked Yuji.

'He likes climbing trees,' Toshie answered for him, taking the cups from the table, 'since he was little.' She walked to the sink at the back of the room. '*Ninja*,' she laughed, ruffling his hair on her way back to her seat.

Hiromi stood up. 'I need to go back to work. Tomorrow I'm free in the afternoon.

Shall we meet here at one o'clock? We can eat together, and then walk. I will finish my story then.'

Junko followed her dumbly out of the door. She turned for a moment, just to check that she'd really been there. Yuji waved goodbye. Toshie was washing the dishes. Junko waved back, thinking, *It's going to be a long time until tomorrow*.

22

Aunt Helen had taken Junko to the swimming pool. It was a Saturday morning, and Peter and Diane were in Japan. Junko always stayed at Helen's when her parents went away. Junko liked those times. Helen talked to her, and read her stories, and played music on her record player. Sometimes they danced around 'like drunks at a Sunday-school picnic', as Helen would say, until they were so dizzy they had to sit down.

Right now they were playing chess, at a table under a big sun umbrella. Junko was winning, and she was only thirteen. Helen was fanning herself with a magazine. 'Good Lord Almighty, I'm hot,' she said. 'You want a Coke?'

'Can I get them? Please?' Junko jumped up.

'OK, sugar.' Helen fished in her bag for some change. 'Here you go.' She handed Junko two quarters and gave her a pat on the bottom as she ran off. Truth was, she was worried about the girl.

Helen couldn't understand her sister any more. She and Peter both acted like Junko wasn't even born most of the time. Oh, they fed her all right, and got her to school. But that seemed to be the limit; it was all they could manage. Junko was a good girl, too. Not moody or demanding, and fun, when you talked to her. Plenty smart. Helen hadn't been able to beat her at chess or checkers for over a year now.

When Junko came back and sat down Helen reached out and squeezed her hand. 'I love you, June-bug, you know that?'

Junko looked into her drink as if searching for a fly.

'Junie? You hear me?'

'I mub moo moo,' Junko mumbled, mouth around her drinking straw. This made them both laugh. *Oh, well,* Helen thought sadly, *at least we can laugh.*

On the way home to Kemah, Helen said, as casually as she could, 'School OK?'

'Yes, ma'am. Fine.' Junko was rubbing Noxzema on to her sunburned arms. They always carried Noxzema to the pool or beach; Junko's fair skin demanded it.

'Everything OK at home?'

Junko stopped her rubbing and looked at her aunt. 'What do you mean?'

'You know,' Helen answered as she steered her old Caddy into the garage, 'teenagers and their parents . . . ' Her voice trailed off. This was no teenage issue and Helen knew it.

Junko shrugged her shoulders and gathered her bag and towel from the back seat. 'Nothing's different.' She tilted her head at her aunt, then put her hand on Helen's knee. 'Is something wrong?'

Helen was inwardly writhing. How could this poor child have adjusted so thoroughly to the way her folks merely tolerated her existence? She couldn't keep the pity out of her gaze. She knew that she was powerless to do anything at all to improve the situation.

Junko's skin itched. The heat of her aunt's concern was intense and suffocating. She opened the car door and headed for the house, hanging her head. She wanted to reassure Helen that everything was all right, but how could she when it wasn't? Junko was so lonely some days that she felt as if she were vanishing, or coming apart, limbs drifting off in different directions.

Helen followed her up the path, which was lined with bright-orange ginger flowers and cool white camellias. A soft warm breeze off the bay was playing in the wind chimes hanging from the front-porch ceiling.

'Can I take a shower?' Junko asked her aunt when they got inside.

'You don't have to ask, June-bug. Go on ahead, sugar.'

Helen put coffee on and sat down to look

at the mail. There was a postcard from Diane and Peter, as usual: *Having a wonderful time. Wish you were here.* The picture was of a geisha, white-faced and lovely, with bowed red lips and a cricket in a cage hanging from her elaborately coiffed hair. The couple were due back on Saturday, three days' time. Helen hated handing Junko over. She wished Junko could just come and live with her in Kemah. But how could she put such a suggestion to her sister? It would be like an accusation.

After pouring herself a cup of coffee, Helen went to sit in her favourite chair by the window at the back. She could sit here watching the water for hours. And when Junko came in with wet hair from the shower, she'd sit between her aunt's knees while Helen rubbed it dry.

23

When Junko got back to the hotel, she was given a message that Gloria had phoned. She had left the name of the hotel with Glory in case her house blew over in a hurricane or something.

It was 3 p.m. in Kyoto, which made it midnight in Houston. Junko hurried to her room to return the call. Glory was a night-owl, and unless she was working a late shift, she'd be watching TV or reading, probably with Bodey on her lap.

'Hey, Gloria? It's me.'

'June! You sound like you're in the next room!'

Junko felt a thrill at the sound of her friend's voice. 'How you doing?'

'We're fine here. Sharon's moved back in.' Gloria and Sharon had split up at Christmas time, but it had always seemed more like a spat than a pitched battle to Junko.

' 'Bout time!'

'Yep. I think we've got it fixed,' Gloria said. Sharon had her head in Glory's lap on the couch, and Bodey was curled up beside them.

'I'm so glad. Tell Sharon I'm glad too.'

111

'I will. Listen, sweetie, Billy's been around here with a message.'

'Yeah?'

'Some gallery in LA wants to mount an exhibition of your work.' Billy acted as Junko's agent, as well as friend and colleague. 'The Green Series, Billy said. I told him I'd call you. It's not till next spring, so there's plenty of time.'

'Wow. That's great. I guess,' Junko added, feeling so far from home that it might take a year to get back. 'I'll call him.' She hadn't thought about pots for weeks.

'What else have you been doing?'

'Well,' Junko answered, thinking, *How do I start?* 'I was walking along a canal yesterday and I saw a Buddhist monk in the sky.'

'What?'

'And Glory, I've met her. Hiromi Mitsuki. She actually approached me!'

'Whoa, girl, you're going too fast. How did she know who you were?'

'She said they knew I'd come. I don't know how they knew, but they did.'

'Weird! Has she said anything about your mom and dad?'

'Not yet. I'm meeting her tomorrow.'

'Oh Junie, that's great. Really.'

'Yeah. Anyway, I'll write and tell you all about it.'

'Great.'

'Tell Billy I'll call him on Sunday, OK?'

'I will. Take care, Junie. Bye-bye.'

Junko hung up the phone. It was funny how distance clarified things. She was discovering that her heart was full of love, not barren and hollow as she'd thought. She loved Gloria. She loved Billy. She loved her Aunt Helen, which she'd always believed she was incapable of, though she'd spoken the words when required to. And it had taken leaving them all to understand this.

24

Junko lay wide-awake in her bed, watching dawn slowly brighten the Kyoto sky. She was thinking.

Simon Magus, in the first century AD, was among the first Christians said to levitate during prayer. Lots of Roman Catholic saints did the same. Saint Teresa of Avila rose a foot and a half off the ground for half an hour at a time during states of rapture. She said there was nothing she could do to stop it. The Brahmins and fakirs in India and the Ninja of Japan did it, and the physical medium Daniel Douglas Home was often observed levitating. In 1868 he was seen to float out of a third-storey window and then back in through another one. He was excommunicated from the Catholic Church as a sorcerer.

Some people could levitate objects, too. Sceptics say that the whole thing's a fraud, and certainly there have been fraudsters. But too many incidences have been witnessed and recorded for the charge to stick. The best possible explanation is the Eastern theory of a universal life force, known as *prana, ki, ch'i* or *akasha*, that belongs to a non-material reality and can manifest itself in the material world.

Junko had never thought much about it. She'd seen the film *Carrie* as a girl, and was just as terrified as everyone else when those knives were flying and that hand came shooting up out of the grave. She loved J. D. Salinger. But for the most part she liked her world to be solid and definable.

Japan wasn't like that, though. It was swirling mist on a mountain lake, or the changing mood of the sky. But it made her feel good, somehow. And seeing Yuji in the air was like a blessing, grace magically conferred. She couldn't wait to see it again.

So she got up early on Saturday and headed for the Path of Philosophy.

As Junko rounded the corner from her hotel, she was surprised by the sight that greeted her. On the wide sidewalk were a band of Japanese cowpokes, three women and three men. The women all wore pale blue suede fringed skirts and matching waistcoats, with checked shirts and cowboy hats hanging down their backs. The men were dressed in denim and raw leather chaps, with cheery red bandannas round their necks. They were singing up a summer storm, Hank Williams' 'I Saw the Light'. They played acoustic guitars, fiddle, mandolin and banjo, and one man was shaking a tambourine. Junko couldn't think of a more incongruous sight.

When they finished the song, the tambourine player grinned garishly in her direction. 'Howdy,' he gleamed. Junko tried a friendly smile but her face seemed stuck. She cleared her throat and tried again, with some success. 'Where are you from?' the man asked.

'Texas. What are . . . what *are* you?' Junko choked out.

The band was starting another song. The man hollered, 'Christians!' as he leaped back into place and began to play. This time it was a bluegrassy rendition of 'Amazing Grace'. She listened until nearly the end, then waved goodbye as she went on her way. There surely was no shortage of fascinating sights in Japan, but that wasn't one she'd been expecting. She had heard that there was a very small Christian minority here. They were considered to be slightly peculiar, when they were considered at all.

Junko was reminded of childhood summers when she was sent to camp at Lake Whitney, way up by Dallas. Her mother knew the woman who ran the camp, Mrs Darlene Truelove. They'd gone to school together. So, even though Junko wasn't a churchgoer, she could be a church-camp-goer, thanks to Mrs T.

Junko loved the camp. She loved the

swimming and boating, and especially the arts and crafts. The singing was fun, around a campfire at night, but Junko was never wholly in the spirit of the songs. She just plain didn't get religion. Her closest friend at camp was EllaJo Berry. EllaJo used to positively writhe during prayers and such. She came from holy-roller stock, though, and it was to be expected. Junko wondered what EllaJo was doing now. Was she a tent preacher, like her mother and father? A mother of five or six by now? Junko felt a pang of jealousy. Some people's lives seemed so clearly laid out for them.

She came to the start of the path. The water was winking at her, a thousand winks a minute. Junko felt bedazzled by it, and sat on a bench. She had plenty of time before one o'clock. *Namu Amida Butsu Namu Amida Butsu*, she was whispering, and *Lord Jesus Christ have mercy on me Lord Jesus Christ have mercy on me*, over and over, until she realized what she was doing and shook herself out of it. What was she trying to do? Levitate? Be Franny Glass? She snorted at herself, and was about to get up when Yuji sat down beside her. She hadn't heard him approaching, and gave a slight jump. Yuji bowed his head.

'*Konichiwa*,' she said.

'*Imouto*,' he answered with a radiant smile.

They sat for some time just looking at each other. Yuji had no need to speak; Junko couldn't think of anything to say. She wasn't sure how good his English was, and besides, he was kind of strange. Finally she said, 'Beautiful day, isn't it?'

Yuji nodded, and took her hand in his. It was warm and soft like a woman's hand. Junko was speechless. They sat there holding hands and staring at the water for what seemed like hours, then Yuji stood and bowed again, and walked off down the path. Junko sat as if entranced, and before long she caught sight of Yuji hanging above the trees, shining like the morning star.

25

At one o'clock Junko walked up the steps to Toshie's front door. She knocked gently and Yuji greeted her with a bow. Junko slipped off her shoes and entered the house, where Toshie was at the stove and Hiromi at the table. 'Konichiwa,' Junko said, nodding in all directions. She felt dizzy, and slightly afraid for some reason. All her life she'd been taught to expect nothing. She'd been lucky, it was true, but she had worked very hard for her success. Now, she was expecting something, but she had no idea what. 'Beautiful day, isn't it?' she found herself repeating, and felt like a fool. The women murmured agreement, each caught up in her task. Toshie was putting the finishing touches to the miso soup and Hiromi was arranging plates of pickles and filling bowls of rice.

Finally they settled down to eating. Hiromi asked Junko, 'What have you been to see in Kyoto?'

'Temples, shops. I love the Path of Philosophy.' She glanced at Yuji. 'I was there this morning.'

'Ah, so,' Hiromi said; 'very beautiful.'

There was silence. Junko asked Toshie, 'May I see your work? Not now, I mean just some time. When you want.'

'Of course,' Toshie answered. 'When we've eaten. My workroom is in the back.' Toshie indicated a sliding screen behind her. 'I sell some in the souvenir shop. Good-luck charms mostly.' Toshie slurped her soup noisily. 'In Japan, there are traditionally no women potters.'

'Huh?' Junko was puzzled.

'Potters are well-known families. Traditional. Men make the pots, women clean up after them. Of course,' she added, 'this was not always the case. Jomon pottery is some of the most ancient and exquisite in the world, and the women made it, like they did in most early societies.'

'I've seen pictures,' Junko agreed. 'I love the Jomon *dogu*, the female figure. Big-headed, broad-shouldered, with tiny breasts and hands. Fascinating. But you work, Toshie, don't you?'

'For myself. And to make some money for Eikando. People come here for luck, when they're taking exams, giving birth, going to job interviews. We have lucky charms for these occasions. My pots,' she added, 'I make because I love doing it. I made the dishes you are eating from.'

Junko took notice, for the first time, of the beautiful bowl she was holding in her hand, and the small, oblong pickle plates, and the ceramic spoons. They were all in shades of green and blue, with different fishes embossed on them in different places. 'Beautiful,' she said; 'they're gorgeous.'

'In Japan, we say a pot is born, not made. You conjure it from the clay; you bring it to life.'

'I know exactly what you mean,' Junko nodded.

'Come.' Toshie stood and beckoned. Junko followed her into the back room. Toshie's space was cluttered with pots in all stages of life: greenware, the unfired creations; bisque, still fragile after the first firing; finished work, with different glazes and carvings, as well as a great slab of watery, grey, unworked clay lying flat on a table. The wheel was in the middle of the room. The smell knocked Junko sideways. In a rush she was back in Montrose, chatting to Billy while she prepared her tools.

Toshie's work was simple, and so fine it took Junko's breath away. A bowl in a cherry-blossom shape seemed to contain the whole tree. A large platter painted with swirls of white and slate-grey might be used to serve up the sky.

121

'This is wonderful stuff,' she said to Toshie. 'Really.'

Toshie bowed. '*Arigato*,' she said. 'Thank you.' She regarded Junko with curiosity. 'Maybe you would like to make something while you are in Kyoto?' she asked, indicating her wheel as an offer.

'Oh! I'm not sure.' Junko stumbled on the words. 'My mind's been totally off clay for a while now. But thank you so much for asking.' Junko walked the perimeter of the room, examining everything on the shelves lined up against the walls. The room was overflowing.

'Shall we go for a walk?' Toshie asked when Junko had finished looking. 'Hiromi is waiting.' Junko followed her back into the living room and they made ready to go. Yuji led them up the hillside, carrying a rolled-up blanket under his arm. When they got to a shady ledge, flatter than the steep path they'd been following, Yuji spread the blanket out and the four of them sat down. It was very hot. Hiromi folded her hands in her lap and began.

'I never knew you existed.' Hiromi looked pointedly at Junko. 'Not until that phone call. I'm sorry.'

'How would you know? I never knew you existed either. My parents were never what you'd call . . . ' she searched for the word. Honest? Nice? ' . . . forthcoming.'

'Like I said, they came here every year. We got to know them quite well. They were devoted to Yuji. But they never mentioned a daughter.'

'Yuji?' Junko was puzzled. 'Devoted to Yuji?'

'Yuji is your brother.'

Was the earth shaking, or was it Junko? She fought to breathe. 'What?' she gasped. 'What did you say?'

'Diane is his mother.'

And so the story was told. Junko never took her eyes off Yuji. Was that her mother's nose? Her cheekbones? Certainly, there was evidence of her mother's love. Junko wanted to vomit, but couldn't move.

The part that Diane and Peter didn't know was this: the dead Junko's brother, Tora, was Yuji's father.

'How do you know?' Junko managed the words with difficulty.

'Yuji told us. He called you *imouto*, sister, on the day you first met. When Tora came here to see me about another of the rape-babies — there were many — Yuji took his hand and said, '*Oto-san*.' Father. So we knew then.' She paused, taking a deep breath. 'I never told your mother and father about this. I didn't think it mattered.'

Junko's head was spinning. She needed a glass of water.

'Are you OK?' Hiromi asked. 'Do you need something?' Yuji moved closer to Junko. As he reached for her hand Junko felt an explosion in her skull. She pushed Yuji away, hard.

'What I don't need is a half-wit for a brother!' she screamed, jumping to her feet. Yuji had recovered his balance, and seemed undisturbed by Junko's outburst. 'And the rest of you — ' Junko's voice cracked here, and she started running down the hillside, tears streaming down her face. She ran out of the temple grounds and along the Path of Philosophy. She ran headlong, tripped on the exposed root of a cherry tree and fell hard, scraping the skin off both knees. She lay in the dirt, sobbing, until a sweet old man knelt over her and asked, in Japanese, if he could help. Junko stood up, brushed the dirt off as best she could, and kept running.

Girl cat, so
thin on love
and barley

Basho, trans. Lucien Stryk

26

It had started to rain, big luscious drops that ran down Toshie's back and prompted her to move from her spot on the hill. Hiromi had already returned home, and Yuji was off on his rambles. He had a pattern of visits he made to other temples and shrines and people. Toshie's plan had been to meditate a while. She was worried about the girl: although Junko was big and obviously strong, she had a frailty about her nature, and the news today would have come as a mighty shock. But what could Toshie do?

She hurried home. After drying herself off, she sat at her wheel to think. The steady rattle and thrum focused her mind.

Toshie had grown up in a tiny fishing village on Hokkaido, the eldest of seven children whose early years had been mostly hard work and hunger, despite the fact that their father was the best hunter and fisherman in the village. By the time she was ten Toshie was expert at gathering seaweed and shellfish from the shore while keeping a sharp eye on her brothers and sisters. The Ainu people were thought to be of Caucasian decent, possibly Siberian, entirely unrelated to the Japanese either racially or culturally. They ended up on Hokkaido due to the aggressive expansionism of the Japanese, who pushed the Ainu into the far northern corner of the country.

Toshie moved to Kyoto after her husband died in the war. She was following an aunt who had married a soldier from Uji, a nearby town known for its green-tea plantation. She had considered becoming a Buddhist monk, but ended up at Eikando making clay charms for the temple. The house she was given had been inhabited by a monk who was a potter, and when he died his wheel was left there. Toshie taught herself how to kick and turn, bringing pots to life from the clay. She kept herself, and Yuji, with the lucky charms — charms for health and love and happiness, for taking exams or going on journeys. But her wheel was her favourite place to be. And though she was childless, apart from Yuji, she bore many beautiful pots.

It was funny, she thought, that Diane and Peter had named their daughter Junko, after the murdered girl. An attempt to honour the dead, no doubt, but which had served as a daily reminder to Peter of his implication in the child's death. And why hadn't they told

Toshie and Hiromi about their daughter? How odd, to keep such a thing a secret.

Toshie's hands caressed the clay into shape. She was making a water jug for the monks' quarters. It was like handling a whirlpool, making a pot, like shaping a tornado. As she kicked and spun, she made a decision to go and see Junko. Talk to her. Explain that all life is suffering. The cause is attachment, desire and ignorance. The remedy lies in detachment, compassion and prayer. If Junko could seek enlightenment, rather than cling on to old hurts, she would be all right. Toshie sighed heavily and stopped kicking. The girl had had a great shock, it was true. But time would help her to adjust.

The jug was beautiful, a simple twelve-inch, big-bellied piece with a thick lip. Toshie ran a wire underneath it and placed it carefully on the shelf. She went to the sink and washed her hands, then slipped into her sneakers and headed for the Kyoto Royal Hotel. She was probably the only woman in Kyoto who wore sneakers with her kimono, but Toshie didn't care. The sun was riding the horizon like an orange thunderball. In an hour it would be dark.

★ ★ ★

129

Junko was asleep, lying on top of the bedcovers, when the phone rang. She got up groggily and winced at the pain in her knees. She picked up the receiver and found that Toshie was waiting downstairs. June invited her up with some trepidation.

'*Konichiwa*.' Toshie bowed as she removed her shoes.

'*Konichiwa*,' Junko replied, offering Toshie a seat at her table.

The two women sat looking at each other for some seconds. It was Junko who averted her eyes first.

'Junko,' Toshie began, 'I know this must be difficult for you. The surprise.'

Junko stood, and winced again. She sat back down.

'You've hurt yourself?'

'I tripped.'

'Can I see?' Toshie leaned forward. Junko stretched her legs out. 'Tsk tsk,' Toshie said, 'too bad. But not serious, I think.'

Junko gave a snort. 'Not serious? Right,' she spluttered, 'I guess I'll live.'

'You'll live,' Toshie agreed.

'No shit.'

Toshie didn't blink at this, but kept staring mildly at Junko.

'Look, I'm sorry. I just — I just guess I'll go home.' Junko suddenly found herself in tears. Toshie moved to Junko's side and put an arm around her shoulder. Junko's sobs shook her body fiercely. Toshie hung on until they had subsided, and then got a hanky from the string bag hanging from her belt. She dabbed at Junko's cheeks, and gave her a gentle kiss on the forehead before sitting back down.

'We have many homes,' Toshie said, 'and not necessarily where we expect them to be.' She stroked Junko's hair. 'Yuji is your brother. He loves you.'

'Yuji loves everybody.'

'Yes. But you are his sister.'

'He doesn't even know me! How can he love me when he doesn't even know me?'

'In Japan, family is very important.'

'In America family is very important. Only some family members are more important than others.' Junko shook Toshie's arm off and went to the sink. She filled a glass with water and drank. She was trying to calm herself, but she was gripped by a terrible, useless rage. The glass cracked as she banged it down on the porcelain, sending a sound like a shot through the room. Both women caught their breath.

The sound of the air-conditioning suddenly seemed deafening. Junko walked back to the table and sat down.

'OK. What do you want me to do now?'

'Come to Eikando tonight at nine o'clock, just as the gates are closing. I'll wait for you at the main entrance.' Toshie stood and bowed. '*Sayonara*, Junko.'

'Bye.' Junko watched the older woman leave the room.

27

When little Junko did a thing her parents disapproved of, they would send her to her room with a look — not a word, but a look so heartbroken and disappointed that it made Junko feel like a monster. Then they wouldn't talk to her for the rest of the day.

Junko got used to solitude, and found ways to fill the time. But she never got over equating spilling a drop of milk with highway robbery, or tearing her skirt with first-degree murder. Crimes against her parents all carried equal weight.

Now, lying on her hotel bed, she couldn't see how she'd ever be able to forgive herself for pushing and insulting Yuji.

She remembered when she'd started high school. Mrs Carney had taken an interest in her work, and it embarrassed Junko. She wasn't used to attention of any sort, apart from Aunt Helen, and praise confounded her. She was nervous, and one day in Art Club, after school, she knocked over a clay-sculpted cat, another student's work. It was greenware, in its most fragile state, when all the water has evaporated and the piece is ready for firing.

The cat shattered. Junko was mortified. She ran from the room towards her locker and her coat and home. Mrs Carney ran after her. She had to pin Junko's hands to her sides to stop her from leaving.

'It doesn't matter, June. Marty won't mind. She's made a hundred of the things.'

Junko couldn't speak. Mrs Carney lifted Junko's chin so that Junko was looking into the teacher's eyes. 'Really, I mean it. It's no big deal.' Junko's lower lip was trembling. She was desperate not to cry. 'Come on back, June. We've still got half an hour.' Mrs Carney put her arm around Junko's shoulders and led her down the hallway.

Junko's feelings at being so easily forgiven were complex. She was shocked to discover that forgiveness was so easy. She was confused about the 'no big deal' part too. Wasn't every moment a big deal? Every word and act a weighty thing? Maybe there was a world where people didn't tread so painstakingly through the days, watching and waiting.

Over the four years she was at Houston High, Junko did learn to relax with her art teacher. She grew to love Mrs Carney's encouragement and support, which had played a major part in Junko's success as an artist.

But that was work. Relationships were a

different matter. She had no idea what her relationship with Yuji should or could be. A brother was a wonderful idea in theory, but the reality of this situation was something else. A brother who was a half-Japanese Bodhisattva, and spent much of his time floating in the air, was too much to take. Especially a brother who had consumed the whole of her parents' affection at Junko's expense.

She rolled over and sighed deeply. The ache in her knees was subsiding somewhat. She'd take a long shower and think hard about how to proceed.

★ ★ ★

Scrubbed clean and patched up, she went down to the dining room for dinner. She was surprised to find Chie there.

'*Konichiwa*,' Junko smiled. 'Back so soon?'

'Howdy.' Chie attempted a Texan drawl but failed. Both women laughed. 'I've got a special order ready. I got here this morning. I could have gone back tonight but I thought I'd see if you were around.'

'Yep. But I have to go to Eikando later, at nine o'clock.'

'Doesn't it close at nine?'

Before Junko could stop herself she'd told

Chie the whole story. Chie's sympathetic gaze and little nods and 'hai's drove her on to the end, and what to do.

Chie sat back and thought a minute. Then she said, 'I think, Junko, that you have a connection here that you weren't expecting, and being connected to people and places is — well, good. Yes?'

Junko waited for Chie to go on.

'Your parents were damaged by their experiences. They let that damage infect their lives, and your life too. It's too bad.' She placed her tiny hand over Junko's. 'But it's over, and what you've got is a chance to . . . ' Chie searched for the right words. 'You couldn't love them. But now you can love Yuji.' Chie paused, shaking her head. 'Is it possible? I'm no expert.'

'But I'm angry. At Yuji, too. At all of them.'

'That's OK. Tell them you're angry.'

Junko sighed, nodded slowly and stood up. 'I'd better get ready to go. See you in the morning? We can go for a walk or something.'

Chie shook her head. 'I'm leaving early. Breakfast?'

'Seven o'clock?'

'Good.' She stood up and gave Junko a hug. 'Whatever happens tonight, you're going to be fine.'

'I guess.' Junko went to her room for her bag and started off for Eikando.

★ ★ ★

The lanterns along the path glowed like small moons as Junko and Toshie made their way to the main temple. This place was so beautiful it made Junko's eyes ache, along with her heart. Kyoto's lights sparkled in the distance, and crickets chirruped in the heat. In August 1995, Japan was experiencing record high temperatures.

They took their shoes off before entering the hall. The *Mikaeri-no-Amida* seemed to be looking over his shoulder directly at Junko. *Come on, Junko, you're dawdling!* She'd read the story in the publicity brochure that was handed to her when she first came here. It seemed like an age ago, but it was only a week! Hard to believe, Junko thought, shaking her head. So much had changed. Or had it? She wasn't sure.

Yuji was kneeling at the altar. Hiromi and Kenichiro knelt beside him. All looked deep in meditation, but as Junko and Toshie came up behind them they turned and nodded a welcome, then stood and beckoned Junko. She approached awkwardly, eyes on her feet. Hiromi took one arm and Yuji took the other,

137

and they walked her on to the temple porch. The view was staggering, with the Higash-iyama hills lantern-lit behind them and the city of Kyoto spread out majestically in front.

Junko detached herself from the gentle grip of her friends. She turned to Yuji first. 'I'm sorry. I didn't mean — '

'*Imouto*.' He took her hand and placed it over his heart. '*Imouto*.' She felt a bright white heat spreading up her arm and through her body, pouring like oil along her veins. She felt transformed. At that moment Hiromi placed her arm around Junko's shoulders and gave her a squeeze. Junko felt invaded by love, swept up in the gush of it. She fainted.

She came to lying on Toshie's futon. She had no idea how she'd got there. Seized by a feeling of terror, she jumped up, grabbed her bag from the floor, slung it over her shoulder and made for the door. There was no one around. She slipped her sandals on and left.

As she climbed on to the bus, the feeling of Yuji's hot hand on her heart seemed to swell up in her mind, crowding into the corners and making it impossible to think. What was happening to her? Some switch had been flicked, some engine started, and she had no idea what power was at work. This was a crazy place. She should move on from here. But where to?

She had a show to put on in LA. Junko would need to work on that. She'd call Billy tomorrow and plan when to come home.

★ ★ ★

When Junko got back to her hotel, it was almost midnight. There was a message that Aunt Helen had called. Curled up on the bed in her *yukata*, Junko dialled her aunt's number and let it ring. It would be 9 a.m. in Kemah.

'Hello?'

'Aunt Helen, it's me.'

'How are you, honey?' Helen asked with delight.

Junko took a deep breath. 'It's kind of a long story.'

'What? What is it?'

Junko went through the whole thing again, sparing no detail until she got to what had happened that very night; she simply couldn't put that into words.

Helen was horrified, and amazed. 'But why didn't she tell me? She could have told me. I just don't get it.'

'I think maybe it was Dad. Maybe he felt responsible and wanted to just forget it. Guilt.'

'We were so close! I don't know how she

could have kept it a secret.' Helen paused. 'But Diane was so different after the war.'

'I wish . . . ' Junko started. 'I wish I'd known her before. What she was like.'

'She was the sweetest little thing.' There were tears in Helen's voice. 'How God-in-heaven awful to have gone through that.'

Junko was nodding, though her aunt couldn't see it. 'Thing is — ' She stopped.

'Go on.'

'Thing is, I don't know what to do. Or how to feel. At first I was really mad, you know, that they'd . . . they'd chosen him. And Hiromi, and Toshie — they were all in on this big secret and there *I* was — '

'Now, sugar, it's probably not — '

'It is. You know they did. Anyway,' she took a breath, 'Yuji likes me. I mean, I think he really loves me.' Junko felt terribly embarrassed.

'Of course he does,' Helen replied soothingly.

'No, no. What I mean is that he wants me to be in his family.'

'Well,' Helen said, 'I guess you are in his family whether you like it or not.'

There was a long pause before Junko said, 'Yeah,' and then, 'I'm gonna think about it. I've got to call Billy tomorrow. Some folks want to put me on in Los Angeles next March.'

'That's great, June-bug. Really great.'

'Aunt Helen?' Junko wasn't used to asking for favours, and took a deep breath.

'Hmmm?'

'Will you come see me out here? Did you get my card?'

'No, honey, I didn't.'

'It'd be great if you could come. I feel kind of . . . ' Junko couldn't begin to describe how she felt.

Helen heard the weight in this silence, and could hardly stand it. 'I'd love to come. When were you thinking?' She started mentally crossing off engagements and promises. Houston could do without her for a while.

'Any time you like.' Junko thought about it. 'Soon,' she added.

'Let me check it out and call you tomorrow. I'll come as soon as I can get organized.'

'Thanks.' Junko yawned. The knowledge that her aunt was on her way sent her suddenly into exhausted relief. 'I'll talk to you tomorrow then.'

'Bye-bye, dear.'

Junko was asleep in seconds.

28

After breakfast with Chie, Junko went to the Yasaka Shinto shrine, near Gion in eastern Kyoto. She loved the bright colours and the crowds of people there, so different from the hush of the Buddhist temples. She walked up to the stone *torii* gates, which were guarded by twin lion-dogs, the *koma-inu*. One dog's mouth is open wide — the *ah* — and the other's is closed — the *un*. The idea, Junko had read, was that *ah* is a baby's first sound, and *un* is the last sound of a dying man. Between those two sounds lies all of creation. In Sanskrit, *ah-un* means 'the end and the beginning of the universe; infinity unleashed'.

Junko walked through the gates and wandered round the grounds. She sat on a rock and pulled her dress up over her knees so the hot sun could do its work. They weren't too bad, really. There had been a dramatic overnight improvement.

Junko mostly wore jeans and T-shirts, but had brought a few cotton dresses along in case she needed them. She felt cool and neat and almost pretty, sitting there in the August heat. It was an odd feeling for Junko, who had spent her life acutely avoiding thinking about how she looked. She'd never worn make-up, and sometimes even forgot to brush her hair. She was an artist, and constantly splattered in clay or glaze or paint. What was she thinking?

She shook her head as if to rid herself of these thoughts, then rose from the rock and turned to leave. As she did so, she crashed straight into a man taller than she was, and nearly as blond. She dropped her bag and covered her mouth with her hands. 'I'm so sorry!' she mumbled through her fingers, staring at him as if she'd encountered a *kami*, one of the thousands of gods that inhabit all things Japanese. Only he wasn't Japanese.

'No harm done,' the man replied. 'Are you OK?'

Junko nodded vigorously. 'Fine. Thanks. I guess I wasn't looking. I'm really sorry.' She bent to pick up her bag, but was so flustered she had to sit down to retrieve it. 'What a mess,' she muttered.

'I think a cup of coffee would do it.'

'What?' This *kami* seemed friendly, and slightly concerned.

'I won't sue — cross my heart — if you buy me a cup of coffee.'

She caught the twinkle in his eye and smiled. 'OK. Deal. Where should we go?' Junko found the words slipping out of her mouth. She blinked and wondered, *Who said that?* She looked at the ground.

'There's a Starbucks around the corner.'

Junko remembered her shock at seeing a Starbucks in Kyoto. But then there were McDonald's and Kentucky Fried Chicken too. It had made Junko sad. She offered her hand as she stood up. 'I'm Junko.'

'Junko? I'm Jesse.' He shook her hand. 'Do you have time now?'

She nodded. 'Yep. Lead the way.'

They walked along the Kamo-Gawa at a leisurely pace. 'Tourist?' Jesse raised his eyebrows. He had broad shoulders and was wearing a brightly coloured T-shirt covered with fish.

'Sort of. Yeah, I'm just visiting anyway. How about you?'

'I teach at a college here. Been here three years.'

'English?'

'I teach English,' he nodded. 'I'm from Vancouver.'

'I've never been to Canada, except for Niagara Falls.'

'Where're you from?'

'Texas. Houston.'

'A cowgirl!'

'More of a cat girl, really,' June laughed. *He's beautiful*, she thought, stealing a sideways glimpse at his face. He was clean-shaven, with wide turquoise eyes, a roundish face and smooth features. He reminded her strangely of Yuji in negative.

They ordered their coffee and took it outside. The tables were crowded, so they sat on a low stone wall, looking over the river.

'How'd you end up in Kyoto?' Junko asked.

'Long story.' Jesse stared at her, as if testing whether to go on.

'Tell it. If you want.'

'When my wife died, I couldn't stand being there without her. So I sold the house and everything in it and started travelling. Had a friend in Tokyo and went there first. I got a job teaching right away. But after a couple of years the concrete got me down. So I moved here.' Jesse's eyes swept the hills. 'This place is fine.'

'What . . . happened?' Junko asked gently.

'Childbirth.'

'I'm so sorry.' Junko searched his face for the level of grief remaining. 'What about the baby?'

'They both died.' Jesse's voice showed no trace of bitterness or anger. It showed no trace of emotion at all, except maybe a slight unease. He cleared his throat and looked down at his coffee. 'It was very sad.'

'Do you have family in Vancouver?' Junko

asked, thinking about her own.

'Yeah. Mom and Dad, and a brother in Montreal. We're pretty close. I get home every year.' He stood up and stretched. 'What about you?'

'I have an aunt in Kemah — that's just outside of Houston.' *And a half-brother in Kyoto*, she thought, but didn't say.

'That all?'

Junko nodded.

'What do you do for a living?'

'I'm a potter.'

'That so? What kind of pots?'

'Jugs are my favourite. Anything, really.'

'What's your last name?'

'Bayliss. It's Junko Bayliss.'

'No kidding! My wife loved your work. She was an illustrator. Kids' books. She spent a lot of time in New York.'

Junko smiled.

'A Japanese name? How'd you get that?' Jesse indicated the river. 'Want to walk some?'

They crossed the bridge to the footpath on the other side. Junko found herself telling her story yet again. She wondered if by telling the story so often she could change it, or affect its eventual outcome. Jesse listened with careful attention. 'Have you had lunch?' he asked when she'd finished.

Junko shook her head.

'Shall we eat?'

'OK. I know where we can go.' She took him to Kenichiro's soba-noodle bar. As Junko slurped noodles from her bowl, Jesse spoke.

'Tell you what.' Jesse's chopstick technique was superb. 'Life is full of surprises. Right?'

Junko tilted her head in agreement.

'It's like they say, if you get a lemon, make lemonade.'

'Right.' She'd heard that one before.

'I think you're still in shock. I mean, we're talking yesterday, aren't we? Before yesterday, your world looked pretty different. Now it's fuller. It's got more folks in it. Which, as long as they're not thieves or psychopaths, is always good.' He grinned. He had a smile as wide as Yuji's.

'What's your lemonade? How did you . . . ?'

'Travel. Learning to look at the broader picture. Japan. Cherry blossom.'

'Huh?' Junko pulled a white-blond wisp of hair out of her bowl.

'The Japanese worship cherry blossom because it represents the transience of life. It comes, it astounds and moves us and brightens our days, and then it's gone,' he snapped his fingers, 'like that. And our job is to lay our blankets on the ground, drink a lot of sake and beer, and have a hell of a good time while it lasts.' He added, 'And besides, there is no end, according to them. You just move from this life to the next one, and on and on.'

Kenichiro smiled broadly at them as he took their bowls away. Junko smiled back. '*Arigato*,' she said, and then, to Jesse, 'I don't know what I believe.'

Jesse caught her eye and held it. 'Yes you do.'

Junko was startled at this. 'Do I?'

He nodded gravely.

Three young teenage girls in school uniforms giggled by. Their skirts were impossibly short, and their white socks bunched thickly around their slender ankles.

'Want to catch a movie some time?' Jesse asked.

'Uh . . . Sure. When were you thinking?'

'Tonight?'

'Can't do it tonight. I've got a show coming up and I've got to make some calls.'

'In Kyoto?'

'LA. Not till next spring.'

'Tomorrow?'

'OK.'

Jesse saw Junko on to her bus just as the sun was setting. While they were waiting, she asked him, 'Have you got a partner?'

'No. After Abby died, I just wasn't interested. Been out with a few women here, but nothing serious. You?'

'Uh-uh. Not for a while.' When was it, she wondered, five years ago, or six? Gary Wheeler, he was called. Her lack of devotion had infuriated him. No, Junko's was a life of very occasional and strictly anonymous one-night stands, which usually happened when she was tipsy, or travelling for work.

They arranged to meet in the hotel lobby the next evening. Junko waved to Jesse from the bus, thinking, *He looks more like my brother than my brother does. And, I wonder if my mother would like him?*

29

When Diane Winkler was a girl, she loved to draw. She impressed everyone with her portraits and still-lifes, done in charcoal or pencil. She'd developed a special technique with an eraser that gave her pictures a smudgy, surreal look while being very accurate at the same time.

But Diane would never have considered pursuing art as a career; she wanted to do something practical, to lead a useful life in her community. So when she finished high school, she joined the Post Office. Athens was a small town, and the man who ran the local PO had just retired — perfect timing for Diane to step into his shoes. She was young, but she was smart and she knew everyone in town. She was also discreet, which folks appreciated. Not that there was much contraband coming in and out of Athens. But rumours could start over the tiniest hint of a Yankee address or a cryptic postcard.

She enjoyed her life; she was content. Living with her parents and sister, she ate well, slept well and had plenty of time for drawing, reading and socializing. There was no man she fancied, but she figured he'd come along eventually, and meanwhile she'd just enjoy life.

One Monday morning Cletus Cleeve, the man who delivered the mail, was sick. Diane did what she had to do in the morning and then locked up and went on his rounds. There was a package to Mr and Mrs Governor Riley, out on the edge of town. Diane headed that way first.

The Riley place was set back from the road. It consisted of a square one-room wooden house set on cinder blocks, and three small shacks ranged around it. One was the outhouse, and the others contained stacks of old magazines, newspapers and junk.

When Diane pulled up, Governor was just coming out of the outhouse, buttoning up his pants. He glared at her and shook his fist. 'What y'all doin' scarin' a man to death like that?' he roared, steaming towards the van. 'I oughta make a formal complaint, goddamn government interfering as usual. What do you want, anyway?'

His wife, Mary, appeared at the front door. She was frail and bruised-looking, with a scarf covering her head. 'What're you yellin' about, Gov'ner? What's the matter?'

'Go on inside, Mary. I'll handle this.' Mary didn't move.

'I have a package for you, Mr Riley.' Without getting out of the van, Diane held out what felt like a wad of magazines wrapped in brown paper. Riley's eyes lit up, but he didn't take the parcel. Instead, he unbuttoned his pants and got his penis in his hand, and started pulling on it while leering wildly at Diane. She was frozen with horror. She felt the package fall from her hand, and its thump on the dusty ground sent her into action. As she put the van in gear the long thin snotty streak of Riley's semen hit the door, just under the window.

As Diane drove off, she could hear the couple's cackling laughter behind her. She glanced in the rear-view mirror and saw Governor holding his sides and Mary slapping her thigh with delight. Out of sight of the house, Diane pulled over and vomited every bit of her breakfast into the ditch. *My God*, she wondered, *what are these people?*

Up until that day in her life, Diane had believed she knew her town and its folks. The discovery that there were perverts amongst them sickened her, and brought with it the idea that much of what she held to be true might not be.

With this scary thought pressing on her mind, she finished the delivery and drove back to the post office. She'd get Cletus to clean the van tomorrow. He was rarely off for more than a day, and it was usually Monday, the weekend's moonshine having taken its toll. But he was a nice guy, Cletus. Wouldn't hurt a fly.

Two weeks later, war was declared. Diane wanted to join up right away, but her parents convinced her that the Post Office was as important as the Army in fighting a war. She fidgeted on until 1943, when she finally left Texas with the WACS. It was a tearful goodbye, and though she didn't know it then, she would never live in Athens again.

30

At 11 p.m. it would be 8 a.m. in Houston. Junko had some time to kill before calling Billy, so after dinner she wrote a letter to Gloria.

Dear Glory,
  This place is getting to me. Seems like all I do is talk and cry, things I never did in Texas.
  Turns out I've got a half-brother here, my mother's son, product of a rape. He's a weird and holy guy. I don't know how else to describe him.
  Poor, poor Mother. She had to leave him here. But I guess she kind of got him back. She had to leave me to do that.
  Can't say more, Glory. Not right now.
  Love to Sharon and Bodey and you too.
  x June

She put the letter in an envelope and stretched out to read some more of her book. But her mind wandered. She remembered when she was about to start kindergarten, and her mother had taken her to buy new shoes. Junko had loved the patent-leather ones with straps and bows and buckles — some even had little flowers sewn on — but her mother had insisted on plain brown lace-ups. 'They'll go with anything,' Diane had said. Junko knew it was pointless to argue.

On the first morning of school, Junko was very excited. She was dressed and ready to go at seven o'clock. Her mother was still in the shower. Junko went into the kitchen and got a bowl from the cupboard and the cereal out of the pantry. She put them on the kitchen table and climbed on to her chair. She placed the cereal carefully in the bowl and reached for the milk. She missed, and the bottle went over. It ran right down into her lap and all over her shoes. Her navy-blue skirt and white blouse were soaked, and the brown lace-ups were a mess. Junko couldn't move for fear.

Her mother entered the kitchen. A look of horror came over Diane's face. She put her hands over her mouth (a habit Junko picked up as the years went by). She didn't say, 'You naughty girl,' or 'You should have waited for me,' or 'Look what you've done!' or even 'Don't worry. I'll clean it up in a jiffy.' She cried. The tears came slowly at first, then ran faster and faster until Diane was sobbing.

Peter came in. He assessed the situation,

and put his arms around his wife. 'It's all right, dear. You go dry your eyes,' he whispered in her ear. He patted her on the back, ushering her out of the kitchen at the same time. When he turned back to Junko, he said, 'Stand up.' He went to the sink and got a cloth, and wiped the mess up from the table and floor before turning to Junko. 'Leave your shoes here. Then go and change your clothes.'

Junko did as she was told. She washed her hands. She got an identical navy-blue skirt and white blouse from her closet and put them on. (Her mother believed a simple school wardrobe was best.) When she got back to the kitchen, Peter was wiping the shoes dry. He handed them to her in silence, his look of reproach burning into her cheeks. She put them on. They were still a little bit wet inside, but she didn't complain.

Her mother, eyes still swollen and red, came in rattling the car keys and swallowing back tears. Junko followed Diane out to the garage and into the car. When they arrived at the school gates, Diane stared straight ahead, waiting for Junko to get out.

'Aren't you coming in?' Junko's voice squeaked out the request. She was desperate. All the mothers would be there on the first day. Wasn't there some kind of rule about it?

'I look a mess,' Diane sniffed. 'Go on in now.'

Junko wanted nothing more than to get out and run in the opposite direction. She sat, hand on the door handle, looking pleadingly at her mother.

'Please, Mother,' she whispered.

Diane wiped her forehead slowly with the back of her hand. Junko opened the door and dragged herself through the gates, squelching slightly as she went.

★　★　★

Now, in Kyoto, she realised that her mother's terror of clutter and gunge was probably part of what had led June into the messy work she'd chosen. Also, that the dressing-down had stuck. Sure, she had to wear sloppy work clothes. But she never dressed up at all. Never adorned herself. She owned almost no jewellery, no hats or scarves or fancy belts like Gloria.

Junko made a decision. Tomorrow she was going to buy a dress.

★　★　★

It was time to call Billy. Junko dialled the number. He picked up on the thirteenth ring.

'Hey, what are you doing?' Junko asked.

'Junie! Did you get my message?'

'Yep. That's why I'm calling.'

'What's it like over there?'

'Fine. You weren't still in bed, were you?' Junko teased him. Billy liked to sleep in when he could.

'Hell no! I was watering the grass before the sun gets too high.'

'Ah. Well, Billy, it's kinda crazy over here right now.'

'Are you OK?' Billy sounded alarmed.

'Yeah, really. I'm OK. But it looks like, I guess it's that — that I'm not exactly who I thought I was.'

'What? What on God's earth are you talking about?'

'It's too long to go into now. I'll write you a letter tomorrow. What about this show?'

'You sure you're OK?'

'Uh-huh. Tell me about LA.'

'Yeah. The Clark Gallery it's called, a new one. They like your stuff and want to exhibit it. They'll also commission a new piece.'

Junko and Billy discussed the details. 'I'll take care of business, Junie. You take care of yourself, hear?'

'I am. So much is happening, but it's all good stuff. I'm pretty sure. Interesting, anyway.'

They hung up. Junko had something solid to work towards. A commission! She'd have to go home to do that. She made herself a cup of green tea and put her feet up. Or maybe, she thought, maybe she could do it here.

31

On her way to breakfast the next morning she was called to the front desk.

'You've just missed a telephone call.' The woman handed Junko a slip of paper. Hideko had phoned. Junko used the desk phone to return the call.

'*Konichiwa*,' she said.

'Howdy, ma'am,' Hideko answered. 'Are you free some time today? Do you want to have lunch with me?'

'I'll only eat with you if it's green food,' Junko said.

'OK. Tsujiri Tearoom, Gion. What time?'

'One o'clock?'

'Good.'

'How's the painting coming along? Am I allowed to ask?'

'Of course! It's fine. But I want to look at you again before I finish.'

Junko laughed. 'You can look all you like. I'll see you at one.' She hung up and went to eat.

After breakfast Junko went on her quest for a dress. Kyoto Station was massive, and crammed with stores that sold everything a person could imagine wanting. She felt overwhelmed by choice, and almost turned back at the entrance. But she forced herself inside and started strolling along the wide gangways, peeking in at endless arrays of hats, scarves, jewels, skirts, tops, shoes and dresses.

After two hours she was beginning to lose heart. Everything was about six sizes too small. But then she spotted a beautiful knee-length silk shift in ice blue, with a cascade of cherry blossoms starting from the waist and getting thicker as they reached the hemline. It looked like it would fit. The dress was narrow at the top, sleeveless, with an oriental collar, but it was fuller at the bottom. It was unusual. She was approached and offered help and she asked to try it on.

She went into a curtained booth and pulled off her jeans and T-shirt. She slipped the cool, luxuriant material over her head and turned to the mirror. She gasped at what she saw. It was as if she'd put on a new skin. The colour brought out the blue of her eyes, and her cheeks seemed to glow with warmth. Her posture was changed, too. She looked graceful and elegant. Junko had never felt graceful or elegant before.

She hurriedly changed and took the dress out to the saleswoman. 'Do you have anything else like this?' Junko asked.

'One moment please.' Maiko (so her name badge said) bowed and went through a door at the back of the shop. She came back shortly with a long-sleeved, tight-waisted creation in midnight blue. The bodice was done in a kind of smocking, with a scooped neck. The skirt was full, and finished mid-calf. 'I think blue is good for you? Your eyes,' Maiko smiled and nodded.

The prices were very high, but Junko liked both dresses, and bought both. She left the station and raced towards Gion.

Hideko was already at the table when Junko arrived. They ordered green noodles and green tofu. Junko showed Hideko her purchases.

'Ah, so! Very beautiful.' She raised an eyebrow at Junko. 'What's the occasion?'

'Nothing.' Junko shrugged her shoulders and cleared her throat. 'I didn't bring many dresses.'

As they ate, Hideko told Junko that the painting was almost finished. They arranged for Junko to go to Hideko's house on Wednesday evening to see it. Yuki would cook dinner.

'So,' Hideko asked, 'what have you been doing?'

Junko shrugged again. 'Nothing much. Sightseeing.' She couldn't bear to go through it all again, even though she was interested in what Hideko might have to say. She'd save it until Wednesday night. Might as well tell the whole family she was related to the weird and wonderful flying monk.

They walked to the bus stop together and said goodbye. 'Wear your dress when you come. My mother will love it.'

'Which one?'

'Either,' Hideko said gaily, gave Junko a hug, then got on her bus. She waved as she pulled away, and blew Junko a dramatic kiss, which sent Junko into a giggling fit. She was still chuckling when her bus came.

When she returned to the hotel there was a message from Aunt Helen. She would arrive at Narita Airport in Tokyo on Thursday morning, and get to Kyoto later that day. Junko was thrilled by this news. Helen would connect it all up somehow, bring the two worlds together. If that was possible.

★ ★ ★

Junko took her time getting ready for her meeting with Jesse. She had a long steamy shower and washed her hair. As she leaned over to rub it dry a thought suddenly occurred to her. *Oh no!* Junko straightened up. *Shoes! What shoes will I wear?* All she had with her were sneakers and a pair of brown leather sandals. It was too late to do anything about it now. She'd have to wear one of the old cotton dresses she'd brought from Houston. Maybe, Junko thought, she'd sabotaged her own efforts. Maybe she even felt relieved.

At seven o'clock she walked downstairs to the lobby. Jesse was sitting on one of the leather couches there, reading a newspaper.

'You can read Japanese characters?' Junko asked, impressed.

'I'm learning. It's tough,' he said as he stood and grinned a greeting. 'Ready?'

'Yep.' They walked out into the evening side by side, two blond giants in a sea of delicate dark miniatures. Many a head turned as they passed. '*Gaijin*,' they heard several times. Junko asked what it meant.

'Foreigner,' Jesse explained. 'Kyoto's pretty cool about Westerners — tourists come here — but out in the country, *gaijin* is usually said with fear and trembling. And very often, abuse.'

'Abuse?'

'You've got to remember this was a closed society until the end of the nineteenth century. Strictly no in-comers. And when the gates finally opened up, people could come, but they could never really belong. Even if they lived here the rest of their lives. Then of course, there's the war.' He took her arm. 'And people away from the cities just don't see many Caucasians.'

The cinema was around the corner from the hotel. They were there in five minutes. 'What are we going to see?' Junko asked.

'*Forrest Gump*, overdubbed in Japanese.'

They got their tickets and went into the theatre.

It was hysterically funny, Tom Hanks speaking Japanese. 'They usually use subtitles,' Jesse said. 'Overdubbing's pretty rare these days. We lucked out!' Junko had seen the movie in Houston, so she knew what was happening. It was, indeed, a rare and hilarious experience.

When the movie was over, they went back to her hotel for a drink. The bar was crowded, but they managed to find a small table in a corner. Jesse ordered two Kirin beers, which appeared immediately before them.

'So.' He took a long sip. 'You haven't seen Yuji since that night?'

Junko shook her head.

'And . . . ?' Jesse let the question hang between them. Junko sighed, and drank, and sighed again.

'My aunt's coming to Kyoto on Thursday. I guess I'll take her to meet him then.' She

165

stared into her glass, then raised her eyes to Jesse. 'I think they're waiting for me to do something. But I don't know what.'

'Maybe they're not waiting at all. Maybe, to them, it's a done deal. Contact has been established. That's enough.'

'It doesn't feel like enough to me.' Her frustration tightened her throat. 'It's about a part I'm supposed to play here. They can't just hang me from the family tree like some mutant among them.'

'Ah,' said Jesse quietly. 'You want this family, I think. Do you?'

'I don't know. Yes. No. I can't afford to imagine what doesn't exist.' She leaned forward and looked squarely into Jesse's eyes. 'If I let him love me, he'll expect something back. And I — ' Junko broke off. She was in serious danger of slobbering self-pity, and making some soap-opera speech about how her mother never loved her. She was a grown woman, for God's sake.

'What would happen if you allowed yourself to just love your brother, and forget about any expectations or consequences?'

Junko was angry now. How could he possibly understand? She shook her head. 'I don't know,' she repeated. That was all she could think of to say.

'Another?' Jesse asked, pointing to her glass.

'No thanks. I'd better get to bed,' she answered, and felt embarrassed at her answer. It was only ten-thirty.

Jesse paid the waitress and they walked to the lobby in silence. Before he left, he took her by the shoulders and said, 'You're a beautiful woman, Junko Bayliss. Goodnight.' Then he went whistling through the door.

32

On Tuesday morning Junko woke with a start. She was sure she'd heard someone calling her name. She stretched and looked around the room, but there was no one there. She ran a hand through her hair, got out of bed, walked over to the window and pulled back the drapes. There, in front of her eyes, was Yuji, suspended in the air, aiming his beatific smile her way. She blinked, and he was gone.

She washed and dressed and ate in slow motion. She knew that she had to go to Yuji, but she had no idea what she would say when she got there. She had to think, but couldn't bring her brain out of the warm mist that was enveloping it.

She wandered along the Path of Philosophy in a daze. It was raining softly now, and Junko had no umbrella, but she hardly noticed. By the time she reached Eikando she was pretty wet, and Yuji stood waiting at his doorway with a towel in his hand. She took it with a nod and entered the house. Toshie wasn't at home.

Yuji sat on a cushion at the low table in the middle of the room while Junko dried her hair. When she had finished, she put the towel on a rail beside the sink and sat down beside him. Several minutes passed in silence. Then Junko found herself talking.

She told him about growing up in a fog of disinterest and numbness and pain. She told him about school, and Aunt Helen, and her feeble and frightened attempts at relationships. She told him about her success as a potter, and her friends, Gloria and Sharon and Billy. Hideko and Chie too.

'My parents — our mother — always resented the fact that I wasn't you,' Junko concluded, feeling utterly drained. 'It wasn't your fault. But when I found out, I was furious.'

Yuji nodded. He had said nothing up to now. Suddenly, he leaned close and kissed her cheek, then leaned back with a satisfied look. '*Imouto*,' he said quietly, 'OK, *imouto*.' Then he got up and left the house.

Junko was dumbfounded. She had just handed her heart into Yuji's keeping, and what had he done but gone and left her there alone. Feeling rattled and confused, she grabbed her bag and went out of the door. The rain had stopped, and so did Junko's heart when she stepped out to see the most perfect rainbow shimmering above Eikando. It filled the sky.

★ ★ ★

On the bus into town, Junko sat next to a middle-aged businessman. He was carrying a leather briefcase, which he held on his knees. He looked startled when Junko settled in next to him, and hugged the window as much as he could, sneaking sly glances in her direction.

'Konichiwa.' Junko nodded hello. The man nodded back. 'Did you see the rainbow?' she asked, hoping he knew some English.

'Rainbow?' he repeated, and shrugged his shoulders.

Junko got her Japanese dictionary out of her bag and flicked through the pages. 'Niji,' she explained, pointing at the sky.

He looked at her as if she were mad, then turned and looked desperately out of the window. 'Gaijin,' he muttered under his breath, and then burst from his seat and went for the door.

A familiar feeling swept over Junko. Her scalp prickled and she hung her head, wanting to disappear. This day was surely going to do her in.

She got off near the station and went in to find some shoes. The first shoeshop she came to had some beautiful bright white leather thongs with tiny cherry blossoms between the

170

toes. Definitely not Junko's style. She bought them without even asking the price. Then she saw some plain black cloth pumps with an open toe, and bought those too. The whole process took fifteen minutes.

As she headed back to the Kyoto Royal Hotel with her packages, she thought of shopping with her mother. Every year in late August, Diane would take Junko to Foley's department store in the Almeda Mall. Diane would choose a pleated navy-blue skirt and a white blouse. Junko would try them on to make sure the size was right, and then Diane would buy five of each, plus white socks and underwear, and then they'd go home. They never got an ice-cream cone or a hot dog or a Dr Pepper. They didn't window-shop or chat, and Junko never got a turn on the mechanical horse. She learned very quickly to walk by the racks of beautiful dresses and mix-and-match casuals and sun-tops in crazy colours and patterns without looking.

When she started high school at fourteen, her mother gave her a clothing allowance and freedom to choose, but by that time Junko's shopping habits were set. She'd buy dark trousers and jeans, and pale tops and sneakers, and not think too hard about it. But she always got a hot dog and a Coke, and loved to sit by herself, waiting for her mother to come pick her up, watching the people coming and going.

Thinking of which, Junko realized: *I'm hungry.* She dropped her new shoes off in her room and headed for a tearoom she'd seen just around the corner from the hotel. She ordered a set menu that was a tofu special: tofu cooked in every conceivable way, like at the Okutan, where she and Hideko had gone after visiting Sanjusangendo. She ate tofu with *bonito* flakes, spring onion and ginger; tofu with sesame seeds and wasabi; miso soup with chunks of tofu floating on the surface; tempura tofu and other vegetables; all accompanied by rice with pickled plums on top. The waitress was brusque but friendly, and asked Junko what her business was in Kyoto.

'I have family here.' Junko's answer came out before she could stop it. Her eyes widened, and the young woman smiled brightly.

'Family in Kyoto? You come here often?'

'Not really,' Junko replied, thinking hard. 'Distant relations.'

'Ah, so. Do you like Japanese food?'

'Very much,' Junko said. 'I love it.'

The woman looked dubiously at Junko. 'Can you eat sushi?'

'I don't know. I haven't tried it.'

'Ah.' The woman was nodding vigorously. 'Many Westerners can't eat Japanese food.' She gathered the dishes from the table and slipped away.

Junko paid the bill and went home for a nap. Suddenly she felt exhausted.

33

When Junko woke up it was dark. The clock beside her bed said 9.30. She stood up and shook her head to clear it, then went into the bathroom and splashed cold water on her face. She'd missed dinner, but she wasn't hungry.

She smoothed her jeans and changed her T-shirt and decided to go to a karaoke bar. Hideko had told her it was something she should see. There was a small one, she remembered, by the river.

As she walked along the busy streets of Kyoto something came to her in a flash, something she hadn't thought about for years but which now made perfect sense. Her mother had been a great knitter and quilter and seamstress. She'd always had something on the go, and it was always in beautiful reds and golds and greens. Socks for Peter, dresses or skirts for Helen, quilts and scarves and gloves for the various charities Diane said she supported. Nothing for Junko, and very little for herself. Diane usually dressed in black.

Little Junko admired these items very much, and longed for some richly patterned thing of her mother's making. But the pieces vanished as soon as they were finished. And now Junko knew where they went: Eikando. Yuji. Of course!

She remembered the time her mother bought a length of cotton in a dazzling print. The fabric was designed in repeating squares, each an intricate mosaic of a million colours. Junko thought it was the most beautiful cloth in the world, and asked her mother if she could have one small square.

'No, June. I'm going to make a dress for Helen, and I'll need all of the material.'

'Just one? Please?' Junko was only five, and hadn't quite caught on to the futility of her position.

'NO.'

The cloth sat there in her mother's sewing cupboard for over a year. One evening, when her parents were playing bridge in the dining room with Molly and Mort Greengrass, Junko crept into her parents' bedroom, and snipped off a square of the material. She made sure to turn the fabric so that her theft wasn't obvious.

She lay on her bed with the soft cotton against her cheek. Dread was already creeping up her spine. What price would she pay for this atrocity? She held the cloth in the air, waving it in the light of her bedside lamp.

She heard her father's footsteps and quickly stuffed it under her pillow as he was opening the door.

'Lights out now, June,' he said, and closed the door again. He hadn't really looked at her, or he would have seen the terrified look on her face.

Junko cried then. Not because of what she'd done, or the punishment she would certainly face, but because she realized that she couldn't keep it. She couldn't hang it on the wall, or show it to anyone. She'd have to throw it away or her mother would find it.

When her sniffles had stopped, Junko looked around the room. Maybe there was a place she could hide it. It was a spare and uncluttered room (at her mother's insistence). But maybe . . . Feeling desperate, she went to her chest of drawers. On top was a jewellery box that her Aunt Helen had given her for her fifth birthday. Junko adored the little ballerina that twirled round to the tinkling tune. She adored the painted wood and the luscious velvet lining. It was her favourite present ever.

She opened the lid. She was pretty sure her folks couldn't hear the music from the living room: they had their own music playing. Junko examined the velvet to see if she could slip the cloth underneath it. She would have to get the scissors from her parents' room.

She opened her door just enough to get through and slipped down the hallway and into their bedroom. The big pinking shears were lying there, but she needed the small scissors. She opened the top drawer of the sewing cupboard as quietly as she could. They were right there, on top. She picked them up, closed the drawer and stepped into the hall. She'd taken two steps towards her room when Molly Greengrass came around the corner. Junko froze.

Molly stood there for a few seconds, needing badly to pee, and appraising the situation. The child looked guilty as sin, but what could she have done? Diane and Peter were so strict with her, she never made a peep most of the time. Molly leaned down and whispered, 'Why don't I tuck you in?' She took Junko's hand and started towards her bedroom. Junko was holding the scissors behind her back.

The cloth! My jewellery box! She'll see! Junko could hardly speak for panic. 'It's OK,' she pleaded, 'I'm going.' Junko pulled free and flew to her door and into her room. She flung herself on to her bed, putting the scissors under her pillow as she did so. Was Molly gone? Would she tell Junko's parents? Junko leaped up and put the scissors and the cloth in her jewellery box. She was careful to place the box exactly where it had been before, so her mother wouldn't notice. She'd try to hide the cloth tomorrow. It was Saturday, and her mother would go grocery-shopping in the morning. Her father would be in the garage, tinkering. She would have time.

It took an hour for Junko to get to sleep that night. But Molly obviously hadn't said anything, and there was no interrogation or telling-off. The next morning she was sleepy but determined. When her mother left, her father was still reading the paper at the kitchen table. Junko waited an agonizing fifteen minutes before he finally took off his glasses, stretched and went to the garage.

Junko opened the jewellery box and examined the lining. It would be heartbreaking to make a cut in it, and she wasn't sure she could do it right anyway. What had she been thinking? With a groan, she closed the lid and took the scissors back to their place. She took the cloth and wadded it up in her hand. She walked into the kitchen, got a brown paper bag from the pantry and placed the material inside. Then she went out the back door and put the bag in the big trashcan. She was replacing the lid when her mother pulled into the driveway.

Junko would like to have buried it, given it a grave. She could mourn it properly then. Visit it regularly. Know where it was. But that wasn't possible.

The giant hammer that Junko imagined would fall from the sky when Diane learned about Junko's crime never came. Maybe Diane never noticed, although she did eventually make the dress for Helen. Maybe she just didn't care enough to get worked up about it. Junko didn't know.

★   ★   ★

The Sakura Bar was jammed with salarymen in their identical dark suits and white shirts, their ties loosened and askew. There were two giggling groups of young office women sitting at tables. A man was singing a drunken and enthusiastic version of 'You Ain't Nothin' But a Hound Dog'. Junko watched him for a minute before approaching the bar. '*Gaijin-chan.*' A man half Junko's height and probably half her weight tried to fling his arm around her shoulders, encouraged by his friends. He only managed to whack her on the back. 'Beer? You like beer, *gaijin-chan?*' Before Junko could protest the man was shoving a bottle into her hand. The men crowded around her like kids at a freak show. She tried a thankful smile, but it came out twisted. Her back was literally up against the wall.

'Sing? You like sing?' the small man asked, waving enthusiastically in the direction of the microphone, where 'Hound Dog' was screeching to a halt.

'No thanks,' Junko pleaded as she was pushed towards the stage. 'Really, I can't sing.' This as the mike was being placed in her hand. She found herself standing above a cheering crowd, her face burning and a version of 'All You Need Is Love' starting up.

'Sing, *gaijin*. Sing!' The little man was positively euphoric.

Junko drank her beer in one huge gulp. She knew there was no way out. She gave a faltering rendition of the Beatles classic, pretty much in tune. She'd never even visited the Texas Corral Club Karaoke Bar, let alone performed in it. 'Nothing you can do that can't be done . . . It's eeeeasy,' she warbled unconvincingly, and brought the house down. The crowd roared and handed her another beer. And put on another song, and another. By her fifth beer, Junko was starting to enjoy herself. It was only her awful rendition of 'Yesterday' that convinced the audience she'd done enough.

As she made her way through the bar, everyone slapped her on the back and said, 'Good!' or gave her a thumbs-up. She was standing at the back when a man who was dressed in leather trousers handed her another drink. He was lean and well-muscled, biceps straining against his tight orange T-shirt.

'Do you come here often?' he asked, arching an eyebrow and giving her a slow, cool wink. There was a moment of silence before they both burst into laughter. Junko was wiping tears from her eyes as she spluttered her response.

'No. Uh-uh. Never been before.' She took a long swig and the room dipped a little. *Better slow down here*, she thought. 'I'm Junko.' She offered her hand.

'Tomoyuki,' he said. 'Call me Tom. Are you visiting Kyoto?'

'Yes.'

Junko learned that Tom was half American, half Japanese. His father was a US Army bigwig who had worked in occupied Japan after the war, under General MacArthur. His mother, twenty years younger than her husband, was from a wealthy Tokyo family. Tom grew up in Tokyo but had moved to

Kyoto for his work. He was a television presenter, most famous for getting celebrities to do crazy things like jump into vats of porridge or walk on their knees for as long as they could. Highly successful, by the sound of it. Top ratings.

When she glanced around the room, she noticed that all the women were very aware of his presence. She should feel flattered, she thought, that his attention was on her. But then, she was a *gaijin* weirdo, after all.

She turned back to Tom and found him staring at her. She cleared her throat and looked into his eyes, which were huge and liquid black. A tingle in her groin surprised her, and she felt heat spreading upwards from it. And he knew it. *I know what you are,* Junko thought, *but what the hell.* She drained her bottle and took his arm.

They went back to the Kyoto Royal and Junko discovered Tomoyuki to be the best lover in the world, and probably all parts beyond. She had never been one to climax easily, but with Tom it was effortless and endless. Mmmmm. After a couple of hours they ordered two bottles of champagne. They toasted Kyoto and Japan and Texas and fucking, and then went at it again. By morning Junko could hardly walk, and she had a terrible headache. Tom was gone. He'd scribbled *Ciao* on a paper napkin. No number, no last name. *But, hey!* Junko thought, *what an incredible night.*

She took two aspirins and went back to sleep, thinking about Jesse.

34

Junko barely managed to rouse herself in time for dinner at Hideko's. She still felt rough, but she was looking forward to seeing the painting. While she was getting ready the phone rang.

'Hello?'

'Hi, Junko. It's Jesse.'

'Hi.' Junko was still uneasy about the other night. 'How're you doing?'

'Fine. I was wondering if you have any time tomorrow?'

'Sure.' Junko paused. 'My aunt's getting in at six in the evening. I've got all day till then.'

'Great. I'll cook lunch for you at my place.'

'That's sweet of you. Thanks. Where should we meet?'

'I'll come and get you about ten. We can take our time then. You can help me cook.'

'Deal. See you tomorrow.'

Junko hung up the phone and rushed for the bus.

★ ★ ★

Hideko was waiting at the bus stop, practically jumping up and down with excitement, when Junko got there. She grabbed Junko's arm and urged her towards the house, saying, 'You didn't wear your new dress!'

'Oh! I forgot. I got up late.' Junko had forgotten all about her new clothes in her hungover state and her scramble to arrive at Hideko's on time. 'All done, then?'

'*Hai*. Another masterpiece by Hideko. Or should I say mistresspiece? Do people say mistresspiece?' She frowned.

'I've never heard anybody say that, no.' Junko laughed. 'Let's just call it 'another superlative work of art, from the hand of a genius'. How's that?'

'Thank you, ma'am. That will do,' she chimed. 'Really, I hope you like it.'

They were greeted by Yuki and Fujio at the door. Junko slipped her sneakers off and bowed. '*Konichiwa*.'

'Come, come,' they beckoned her furiously with that go-away motion that tickled Junko so much. She followed them into Hideko's studio, where the painting stood covered by a cloth. It was four feet tall and about three feet wide, Junko guessed. They were all holding their breath.

'Ready?' Hideko asked.

'*Hai, hai, hai*,' the others answered, and

185

Junko added, 'Let's see it!'

With a flourish, Hideko swept the drapery away.

What Junko saw was not so much the gorgeous capturing of the light filtering through the window, or the surreal little frog in mid-hop above the pond. It wasn't so much the beautifully muted pale greens and whites and creams and golds. It wasn't her figure, long and wiry but with a touching softness about it too. It was her face. Partly in profile, Junko seemed to be looking both out into the garden and into the room, or somewhere in between. Hideko had captured such longing in her eyes that Junko was stunned. She sat down on the wooden chair and tried to breathe. Was this how she appeared to the world?

'Beautiful, *ne?*' Yuki said softly, and sucked her teeth.

'So beautiful,' Fujio agreed, nodding.

Junko jumped up, ran to the toilet and puked.

When she came out, several minutes later, Hideko and her parents were sitting around the dining table. Hideko jumped up and ran to Junko. 'Are you all right?' she asked breathlessly. Junko gave a nod. 'I'm so sorry, sorry. You don't like my painting?'

'I do, really. But I . . . ' Junko tried to

explain. 'I look so . . . so lost.'

Hideko indicated the table and Junko sat down on the cushion provided especially for her. (She wasn't sure she'd ever get used to sitting on the floor all the time.) Hideko sat next to her and placed a hand over Junko's. 'Ah, so. But,' Hideko said, 'we all look lost sometimes.'

Junko looked up and found the Tanakas all inclining intently in her direction, brows furrowed. She buried her face in her hands and took a few deep breaths to stop herself from crying. Then she straightened up. 'I just didn't realize it was so obvious.'

'No, Junko. Hideko is a painter. She sees more than others see, *ne?*' Fujio said carefully. 'Do you understand?'

'It's different!' Hideko exclaimed. 'No ordinary portrait!'

'It's a beautiful painting, I agree. I'm very grateful, really. I guess I don't see myself so well when I'm brushing my teeth, which is about the only time I look in the mirror.' Junko tried to laugh.

'Please eat,' Yuki said, standing up. 'It's ready.' She went and got giant prawns and rice and some kind of greens with an egg stirred in and, of course, lots of pickles. They ate.

'My aunt's coming from Houston tomorrow evening. I'd love you to meet her,' Junko said over green tea. 'Will you be my guests for dinner one night? You could come to the hotel. Or another place?'

'No, no,' they answered. 'You must bring her here.'

'Please,' Junko replied, and it went back and forth like that for a while. Japanese courtesy could be exhausting. 'I'd like to see another restaurant in Kyoto, somewhere different. With you as my guests,' Junko insisted.

Yuki looked at Fujio, who looked at Hideko, whose eyes lit up. 'I know! Okutan, if you don't mind going again. I think your aunt would find it interesting.'

So it was settled. They would go together on Saturday evening, then bring Helen here to see the painting.

'I'm sorry, Hideko,' Junko said as they walked to the bus stop. 'Please say sorry to your mother and father. I overreacted.'

'It's OK,' Hideko waved her arm. 'My work is sometimes shocking!'

'I love the frog.' Junko smiled at the thought. 'Unreal.'

'The world is a crazy place.'

They ran the last few yards, as they saw the lights of the bus heading their way. A quick hug and Junko was off. She stared at her blurred, unreal reflection in the window the whole way home.

Drizzly June —
long hair, face
sickly white.

Basho, trans. Lucien Stryk

35

Jesse was waiting when Junko got to the hotel lobby the next morning. As they walked out into the sunshine together, Jesse took her hand. Junko was surprised at the ease of this; the last time she'd walked down the street holding hands with someone it was her mother, and that had been rare enough. But it felt OK. Jesse was a natural hand-holder. There was nothing portentous or demanding going on, maybe just a little bit of sweet fizz between them.

'I live in western Kyoto,' he said, 'in a big apartment block. Great neighbours.'

Junko thought of Gloria and Sharon. 'Me too. I mean, great neighbours. I've got a little house.'

'The Japanese seem to relish being piled on top of each other. Even out in the sticks, where there's space, they still build everything close-to.'

'In Texas we like space.' Junko smiled.

'Oh give me land, lotsa land under starry skies above, don't fence me in,' Jesse sang, and Junko joined in. 'Let me ride through the wide open country that I love,' and so on, all the way to the bus stop, still holding hands. Junko felt like a child, which she'd never felt when she was one.

They climbed aboard the 93 bus. It was jammed with people, and they had to stand, squashed together, for the thirty minutes it took to get to Jesse's place. Junko found herself leaning her head on his shoulder, which was not uncomfortable.

The buildings were tall and modern, surrounded by gardens with cherry trees, pines and Japanese maples. They took an elevator to the fifth floor of Building Four. Jesse unlocked his door and bowed slightly, inviting her in. She fumbled with one of her sneakers in the entranceway; Jesse leaned down and untangled the knot, then slipped the shoe off for her.

'Prince Charming or what?' she laughed, blushing as his warm hand cupped her heel.

'Ever at your service,' he answered, leading the way into the main room.

It was not a big place, but it was lovely. Unlike Hideko's house, it had two sofas, plus a dining table with chairs. The floor was carpeted, and there were a million books on shelves. The tiny kitchen adjoined the living room, separated only by a counter.

'Coffee?' he asked.

'Uh-huh, thanks.' Junko was examining the

books. '*Franny and Zooey*,' she said, 'that's my favourite book in the world.'

'Great stuff.'

Junko went to the window and looked out. She could see forested hills for miles. It was a beautiful view. She turned back to the table as Jesse was putting the coffee down. 'Milk?' he asked, setting a carton on the table.

'Black.' She sat down and picked up her cup. 'Smells great.'

'So,' Jesse said, 'any decisions?'

'I went to see Yuji on Tuesday.' Junko shook her head. 'I'm not sure what happened.'

'What do you mean?'

'Well, I told him about — my life, I guess, and how he'd come as such a shock to me. But how it all made sense, in a way. Looking back.' Junko sipped her coffee.

'Yeah?'

'Yeah. And then he left. He just left me there. But, you'll never believe this. When I walked out of the house there was the most amazing rainbow. And everything seemed OK then.' She shook her head again. 'Do you know what I mean?' She looked into Jesse's blue-green eyes. *Like the sea*, she thought, *just like the sea.*

'I think so,' he replied. 'Sounds like a pretty amazing guy.'

'Yeah, he is.'

Jesse stood. 'I'm going to start cooking. Would you like a drink? I've got a duty-free bottle of Bourbon I haven't even opened yet.'

'Why not?' Junko stood up and went back to the window. Jesse joined her there with two straight shots in crystal glasses.

'Bottoms up,' he grinned, and they drank before sitting down together. 'I'll leave lunch for a few minutes, OK?' He poured two more shots.

'Are you planning to stay here? In Japan, I mean?' Junko heard the heat of the whiskey in her voice.

'For now. It suits me fine. The money's good, and I like the people. I have time for my own work too.'

'What's that?'

Jesse poured again.

'Poetry.'

A poet, Junko thought. *Of course*. She chuckled.

Jesse looked mildly offended. 'What's funny?'

'Sorry,' she said, trying to straighten out her smile. 'It's just, I come to Kyoto, become an artist's model, find a Japanese brother and a Canadian poet whose dead wife loved my work.'

Jesse flinched. Junko's hands flew to her mouth. 'Oh, sorry. Really, really — ' He stood up but Junko grabbed his hand. 'Please, Jesse, I don't know how to — to do anything right.' She tugged, and he sat back down. Junko was still holding his hand, and she knew, absolutely, that she had no intention of letting go.

Two drinks later they were in bed. Fast work, but this seemed serious, and slow, and more loving than Junko could take, almost. When he started to get up and fix lunch, she held him tight for a minute, resting her cheek in the crook of his arm.

'Hey.' He took her St Christopher medal in his hand. 'Very nice. Did you make it?'

'No. My friend Billy did. A going-away present.'

'Who's Billy?'

'My studio's in his gallery. Look, Jesse, this is . . . I'm not used to thinking very hard about these things,' she said.

He took her chin and lifted it, which she didn't resist. They looked at each other squarely. 'You could try to get used to it. OK? What do you say?'

What does he mean? Junko thought, suddenly panicked. *I hardly know him.* She didn't answer, and he jumped out of bed, whistling.

'What's your last name? I don't even know your last name,' Junko said.

'Glass. Jesse Glass,' he answered, grinning, 'just like Franny and Zooey.'

'You're kidding! Seriously?'

'That's me!'

Jesse grilled the tuna steaks he had ready and they ate. They decided to go to meet Aunt Helen together.

36

The *shinkansen* was on time, as trains always are in Japan. Aunt Helen came gliding down the platform towards them, pulling a medium-sized leather suitcase behind her. She looked as elegant as ever, silver hair swept up and held with a turquoise and silver clip, and not a sign of jet-lag or fatigue.

'June, dear,' Helen said, embracing her niece. 'Who's this?' She nodded at Jesse.

'This is Jesse Glass. Jesse, this is my aunt, Helen Ellis.'

'Pleased to meet you,' Helen said as Jesse took her suitcase. 'You could be brother and sister!'

Junko gave an embarrassed laugh, but Jesse liked the idea. 'Come on, sis,' he said, 'let's catch a bus.'

Jesse saw them to the hotel and then went home. They'd meet tomorrow at Eikando.

Junko had reserved the room next to hers for Helen. She sat on the bed while Helen unpacked her things. 'How long will you stay?' she asked, stretching her arms over her head. She could still feel Jesse's skin against hers, and it gave her a little shiver.

'Ten days. There's a charity performance of the Houston Symphony Orchestra I've got to get back for.' She paused. 'Are you in love already?' Helen asked. 'Sure looks like it.'

Junko blushed. 'He's nice, isn't he?' She threw herself back on the bed. 'Oh, Aunt Helen. It's way too soon. I don't know.'

'Yes you do.' Helen looked pointedly in her direction.

Junko sat up again. That was exactly what Jesse had said. Maybe she knew more than she thought she knew.

'I haven't been here two weeks yet, and already it feels like my life has changed completely.'

'Maybe it was changing all along. Maybe everything you've ever done was to serve the purpose of getting you here.' Helen sat down next to Junko. 'Ever thought of that?' She put her arm around Junko's waist. 'I'm famished,' she added.

'We can eat here, if you want. The food's great.'

They went to the dining room and ordered. Junko filled in the gaps for Helen, and told about her last talk with Yuji. Helen listened intently, then asked, 'When can I meet him?'

Junko looked at her watch. It was eight-thirty. 'The temple closes at nine, but we can go to the house anyway, after we've eaten. You're not too tired?'

Helen shook her head. 'He's my nephew, after all.'

These words burned, somehow, and Junko suddenly felt afraid. She gripped the table, and Aunt Helen leaned in and grabbed her hand. 'Not like you, June-bug. Not at all. You know that.'

It didn't help. Junko was seized with panic. What if Yuji stole her aunt's love too? Maybe this wasn't such a great idea.

'June. He's family, and that's important. But he didn't grow up with me. I didn't take him to the beach or the library or the movies. I didn't love him from birth. Come on,' she squeezed Junko's hand, 'it's OK.'

'Sorry.' Junko forced herself to breathe out. How could she think her aunt would abandon her, like her parents had done? Helen was made of better stuff than that. But Yuji was cunning — no, he wasn't cunning. He was just lovable.

'Don't be sorry. I love you best in all the world, June, and you know it. But I'll tell you as often as you need to hear.'

They finished their dinner and went to the temple. Yuji was waiting at the gate, which surprised Helen, but Junko said, 'He's always doing stuff like that.' They followed him to the house, where Toshie was preparing green tea.

'*Oba*,' Yuji said, and placed his hand on Helen's heart, his bright smile like a crescent moon.

'Must mean aunt,' Junko said. 'I'm *imouto* — sister.'

'That's right,' Toshie said as she brought the tea to the table. They sat down, and Toshie poured.

'Toshie, this is Helen, my mother's sister. Helen, this is Toshie, who Yuji grew up with. She's a potter, like me,' Junko added, even though Helen already knew. The women nodded at each other and they drank their tea.

'My sister never told me about Yuji,' Helen tried to explain, the pain obvious in her voice, 'or I would have . . . well, I don't know what I would have done. Come to see him, at least. Helped out.'

Toshie nodded. 'You did help, I think, with Junko. Diane and Peter set up a fund for Yuji early on, so he will always be provided for. The temple would keep him in any case. But the money helps the temple too.' Toshie shook her head. 'They were very generous.'

Junko winced. 'They could afford to be,' she said sharply, and then regretted it. Yuji never stopped smiling.

They finished their tea in somewhat

strained silence, and Junko and Helen stood to leave. Yuji walked them to the bus stop and waved when they pulled away.

'Doesn't say much, does he?' Helen said.

Junko laughed with relief. 'Nope. He sure doesn't.'

'Nice smile, though. No match for yours, of course.' They rode the whole way home arm-in-arm.

37

At noon on Friday, Helen and Junko met Jesse at Kenichiro's soba-noodle stall. They got their food and sat eating in the shade.

'So, Jesse, are you planning to stay in Japan?' Helen enquired.

'My plans,' he answered, with a glance at Junko; 'who knows?' He waved his chopsticks. 'I love this country. But a *gaijin* — foreigner — can never really belong in Japan. People who've lived here all their lives, but whose grandparents came from China or Korea, are still *gaijin* here.' He shrugged. 'It sort of suits an outsider like me. But I've taken a fancy to your niece, and I'm prepared to be where I need to be to see what happens with that.'

Junko dropped her chopsticks with a clatter. 'A *week*,' she said. 'It hasn't even been a week!' Was Jesse really saying he was willing to organize his life around hers?

'What are your plans?' he asked gently.

Jesse's implication that she had nothing else to look forward to infuriated and flustered Junko. 'I'm not sure. I have a commission. I could go home, or I was thinking, I could maybe do it here. If Toshie'd let me use her wheel.'

This could be perfect, Helen was thinking, *just perfect. They look like they were made for each other.* She was also aware of her long-held, desperate desire to see Junko settled and happy. The girl seemed at times to be haunting her own life. 'What a lovely idea,' she said. 'Would you stay in the hotel?'

'I guess so. I haven't thought it out yet.' She shook her head. 'Jesse, I'm not an easy person, you know. Aunt Helen'll tell you. Won't you?' She looked pleadingly at her aunt.

'You just weren't ready, June. Maybe you're ready now.' She patted her niece on the back. 'Give it a whirl, why don't you?'

'Give it a whirl, Junko,' Jesse repeated, nodding vigorously.

Junko felt trapped. All this positive thinking was wearing her out. She'd fail or she'd run, like she always did, she was sure of it, and Jesse would end up hating her for it. It seemed OK yesterday to take it slowly, see what happened without making any promises. A public commitment was a pressure she couldn't abide.

'I don't feel so well.' Junko stood abruptly and grabbed her bag. 'I think I need to lie down. Jesse, will you show Aunt Helen the grounds, and the Path of Philosophy or something? And get her back to the Kyoto Royal?'

'Sure.'

'I'll see you back at the hotel,' she said to Helen, and left.

As they watched Junko hurry away, Jesse said, 'I don't want to scare her off.'

'You're not the one who's scared her off. That happened a long time ago.' She looked at Jesse. 'Please, please stay with it. It might be tough. But it'll be worth it.'

'Right.'

They got up and walked the afternoon away, thoroughly enjoying each other's company.

★ ★ ★

Junko entered her room just in time to vomit in the sink. The bus ride had made her feel even queasier. *This is weird*, she thought, *twice in three days. Maybe I've got some kind of bug.* Or the stress of the situation was doing her in. More likely it was stress and anxiety.

She lay down on her bed and fell immediately to sleep.

She awoke five hours later to a gentle tapping on her door. 'June? It's me,' Aunt Helen said softly. 'Are you all right?'

Junko stumbled to the door and let her aunt in. 'I fell asleep,' she yawned. 'What time is it?'

'It's about six o'clock. Are you hungry?'

'I think so.' Junko clutched her belly. 'I was sick.'

'Oh dear.'

'I feel OK now.' She went into the bathroom and rinsed her face, then brushed her teeth. She ran a comb through her hair and went back into the room, straightening her dress as she did so. 'Ready.'

In the lift, Helen asked, 'Is it a bug, do you think?'

'I'm not sure.' Junko shrugged. 'My appetite seems OK.'

They ate quickly and quietly, and went back to Junko's room to watch Japanese television. Tomoyuki's show was the funniest. Junko didn't tell her aunt about Tom; it wasn't necessary. Here was a man who encouraged famous people to walk around the studio set with their toes tied together to see who'd fall over first.

They turned the TV off and sat drinking green tea and looking out of the window at Kyoto's busy, twinkling streets. The bright white sign of the Hotel Marion shone like a new constellation in front of them.

'I'm so glad you came, Aunt Helen.'

'I've always wanted to come to Japan. Something about your mother's obsession put me off the idea, though. I guess it seemed like her place, not mine.' She looked at Junko's profile in the darkened room. 'Thanks for asking me.'

Junko breathed deeply and audibly. 'So much to take in.'

'I wish Diane had told me.' Helen pounded her fist on her thigh. 'To carry all that with you, all those years . . . '

'She had Dad.'

'Yes,' Helen agreed, 'that she did.'

They watched the neon night until Helen's eyes began to droop, and she went to her room to sleep.

38

Junko decided to cheer herself up by wearing her new dress, the pale blue one with cherry blossoms. The white sandals looked fine with it.

Aunt Helen was still asleep — catching up, Junko supposed, from the journey — so Junko went by herself for her breakfast, after slipping a note under Helen's door to tell her where she was.

To her surprise, Jesse was sitting in the lobby when she walked through. She went and sat down beside him.

'Do you want some breakfast?' she asked. 'I'm just going for mine.' Jesse followed her into the dining room. 'Thanks for keeping Helen company.'

'No problem. Are you OK?'

Junko nodded. 'But I was sick when I got back here. Maybe something I ate.'

'Maybe something I said?' Jesse asked. 'Junko — ' he started, but she cut him off.

'Time, Jesse. Just time. I don't want to make a promise I can't keep. In fact, I don't want to make a promise at all.'

'No. Fine by me. No promises.' He leaned

back and grinned. 'You're looking particularly lovely today, Ms Bayliss, if I may say so.'

Junko suppressed a laugh. 'Stop it!' she said through a mouthful of muesli. She managed to swallow, and put her spoon down. 'I got a new dress.'

'It suits you.'

Junko smiled. Maybe it would be OK. Jesse seemed like a good guy, and wouldn't push. 'Thanks.'

Helen joined them. 'Sleep well?' Junko asked.

'Gloriously,' she answered. 'What's the plan for today?'

'We're having an early dinner at Okutan with Hideko and her parents. Then we'll go back to their house and you can see the painting.' Junko looked at Jesse. 'You want to come?'

'Sure,' Jesse answered. 'What about this morning?'

'I want to talk to Toshie.' Junko looked at her watch. 'It's almost eleven already. Where did you two go yesterday?'

'The Path of Philosophy. Then we went to Sanjusangendo,' Jesse replied.

'Exquisite,' Helen said, 'and so moving.'

'I felt that too,' Junko nodded. 'Unbelievable. What would you like to do today? More temples? Shops?'

'I'm quite happy to go back to Eikando, if that's what you want to do. I could spend hours there. There'll be time for the others.'

'Tell you what,' Jesse began: 'school starts again on Monday. There are a few things I need to do this afternoon. What time are you going to Okutan?'

'Five.'

'I'll meet you there.'

They parted then, Jesse heading off on his errands, Junko and Helen to Eikando.

★   ★   ★

'What's this about, going to Eikando?' Helen asked Junko on the bus.

'I want to have a good look at Toshie's wheel. Maybe I can work on my commission here.' Junko gazed out of the window at the bustling crowds. 'I like Kyoto. But I'm not sure. I'm used to my own place.'

'You might surprise yourself.'

'Yeah,' Junko agreed. 'That's possible.'

'And Jesse?'

'Come on, Aunt Helen! I hardly know him.' Junko squirmed in her seat.

'He's a nice guy.'

'Seems so.'

'It'd be nice to get to know him better, wouldn't it?'

'Yes. It's just that I always . . . I never have been able to go the distance, with anybody. I'm afraid it's too late now. I always mess it up.'

'Oh, June-bug. It's never too late. And things have changed, haven't they?'

Junko thought about this before replying. 'I thought they had. I'm not so sure any more. Mother and Dad are dead. That's a change. But I hardly saw them anyway. And this grief is not very different from the grief I've always felt where they're concerned.'

'And Yuji?'

'Yuji.'

'He's your kin.'

'Yes. Our DNA has similarities. But that's about it.'

'But June — '

'Well, what difference does it make? He has his life and I have mine. Period.' Helen looked worried, so Junko took her hand and added, 'It's all right, Aunt Helen, really. I'm going to keep seeing Jesse, and see what happens. Just take it slowly, that's all.'

Helen gave her a sad smile, which prompted Junko to say, 'He is nice. And easy, he's so easy! Right from the start there was something . . . ' she searched for the word, 'something pretty natural between us.'

They got off the bus and walked up the

path to Eikando. Toshie was making rice balls when they arrived at the house. Yuji wasn't around.

'*Konichiwa.*' Junko bowed and slipped off her sandals. Helen did the same.

'*Konichiwa.*' Toshie returned the greeting and the bow. 'Please, sit down. I'll make some tea.'

They settled themselves on the floor around the table. Toshie brought a teapot and three small bowls. 'How lovely,' Helen said, examining the bowl in her hand. 'I love the colours.'

'*Arigato.* These are my favourite.' The pot and bowls were a rust red, with pale-green swirls and what looked like small puffy white clouds. They drank their *cha* and talked about the weather, which was sweltering, and the fact that next week it would be September and maybe it would soon start cooling off. 'Will you stay for a while?' Toshie asked Junko, 'to see the *kouyo*?'

'That's when the Japanese maples go red,' Junko explained to Helen. 'I'm thinking about it,' she replied, 'and I was wondering, could I have a look at your wheel? Is the offer still open?'

'Of course.' They went into the back room. The wheel was set up with a piece of clay ready to turn. 'Please,' Toshie said, 'try it.'

Junko sat down and took the clay in her hands. She used an electric wheel at home, and it took her a few minutes to get used to a kick-wheel again. But it came, and soon she was riding a whirlwind, the best feeling in the world.

When she had pulled and pushed and spun several different shapes from the clay, Junko slowed her kicking and flattened it into a blob again, then placed it on the counter to rest, ready for Toshie's hands. Toshie was holding a damp towel out when Junko stood up. She wiped her hands thoroughly and gave it back with a nod.

'It's a great wheel, Toshie. Thanks a lot.'

'*Doh itashi mashtay*. You are welcome, anytime.'

'This is beautiful, Toshie,' Helen said, having examined every piece in the room while Junko was at the wheel. 'June, couldn't you get her something in the States? If women can't be potters here, I mean. This is striking work.'

'I am too old now,' Toshie laughed, 'and I wouldn't leave Eikando anyway.'

'You wouldn't have to,' Helen said. 'June could arrange it for you.'

Toshie shrugged. 'The world outside means very little to me. I make pots for myself, and the monks.'

'Toshie,' Junko began.

'*Hai?*'

'I have a show coming up in the spring,' Junko spoke slowly, 'and a commission to make some pieces for it. If I stayed on in Kyoto, could I use your wheel on a regular basis? I mean, a couple of hours a day or something?'

'*Hai*. Of course.'

'*Arigato*.' Junko bowed, feeling a strange elation. 'I'm very grateful.'

Helen and Junko said goodbye and made their way to eastern Kyoto, the old town, where Okutan was located. They took their time, looking in the bright and tempting souvenir shops as they climbed the steep road to the restaurant. Helen bought some Japanese sandals with wedged wooden soles and velvet straps. Junko finally found a present for Billy: a carved wooden chilli pot full of 'seven-spice' seasoning, which Junko liked on her soba noodles. Billy was a lover of jalapeños, habaneros and Tabasco sauce. He'd like this stuff. The pot was made in the shape of a chilli pepper, like Kenichiro's but much bigger.

As they strolled through the crowds, Helen asked, 'Do you think you could do something with Toshie's work?'

'It's outstanding, isn't it? I've thought

213

about it, but she doesn't sound interested. I wouldn't want to bring the American art-loving public into her life unless she wanted me to. Might be hard on her. And Yuji.'

'Hmmm,' was Helen's response, 'maybe.'

They got to Okutan at five o'clock. Hideko had made a reservation, and Helen and Junko were shown to their table, where the Tanaka family were waiting.

'*Konichiwa*,' Hideko greeted them. 'Please, sit down.'

'I've invited a friend. I hope it's OK? I thought you'd like to meet him.'

'No problem!' Fujio exclaimed. 'Where is he?'

'Late, I guess. This is my aunt, Helen Ellis.'

'Pleased to meet you,' Helen said, settling herself on to the floor.

Fujio told the waitress to set another place. 'How was your journey?' he asked.

'Nice, but a long one,' Helen answered. 'I hear you make the trip a lot.'

Fujio nodded. 'My company has an office in Houston.'

'You'll have to come and visit me when you're over there next.'

'Thank you. It would be my pleasure,' Fujio nodded. 'I will bring my wife.' He turned to Yuki. 'Yuki-chan, will you come to Texas?'

'*Hai*,' she answered. 'We have discussed this many times. But now I know someone

214

there, it will be better.'

The food started to arrive, wave after wave of tofu and vegetable dishes, noodles and rice. Junko and Helen worked on their chopstick skills, and were constantly complimented by the Tanakas. '*Jozu desu ne!*' they exclaimed, over and over, 'How clever!', which was embarrassing to Helen, as she was only about 50 per cent successful in getting the food anywhere near her mouth, let alone into it. She ended up asking for a fork.

As they ate, Junko told the Tanakas about finding her brother.

'Ah, so!' Fujio exclaimed. 'Everybody knows Yuji!'

'Yes,' Junko said. 'That's what they say.'

'A sad story, but a happy ending, I think,' Yuki said.

'You have a Japanese brother,' Hideko chimed. 'You're one of us!'

They ordered sake and made a toast to family and ancestors and blood that defines you and makes you real. Junko took several pictures with her new camera: she got one of Hideko and her parents, one of Helen and Hideko, and one of all of them. She got the waitress to take one with Junko in it too. They got along just fine, and by the time the tofu ice-cream arrived they all felt like old friends. Except for Jesse, who never showed up.

39

Back at the Tanakas', Yuki made *cha*, and Helen went with Hideko and Junko to see the painting. Helen couldn't repress a little gasp as the picture was unveiled.

'Oh my my,' she whispered, shaking her head. 'You've really got her, haven't you?'

'I think so,' Hideko replied.

Helen felt the sting of a tear, and blinked it rapidly away. 'June, my dear,' she started, but Junko interrupted her with an uneasy laugh.

'That's what I look like, then,' she said ruefully.

'No! Not always. But sometimes, yes. Since you were a child. It used to make me feel so helpless.'

'I know.' Junko looked down at her big feet and sighed.

'It's a beautiful portrait, Hideko. What will you do with it?' Helen asked.

'Keep it with my other work for now. My teacher says I can have a showing when I'm twenty-three. Three years from now.' She looked at Junko. 'He owns a gallery in Tokyo. He likes this picture very much.'

Junko winced at the thought of her despair

being on public display. But she said nothing. Three years was time enough to think what to do.

They went back into the living room, where Yuki was pouring the tea. They settled around the table and Yuki asked, 'What happened to your friend? I forgot all about him.'

Junko shrugged. 'Something must've come up.' She did feel unsettled by Jesse's non-appearance. What could have happened? Maybe he was just standing her up. He'd be right, she thought, to get out now, before it had the chance to get messy.

'Who is he?' Fujio asked.

'He teaches English here. He's Canadian. I met him at the Yasaka shrine.'

'Ah, so. Many foreigners teach English in Japan.'

'Hmm,' she agreed, 'he said that.'

Helen and Junko told the Tanakas about Kemah and Galveston Island, neither of which Fujio had seen yet. He and Yuki said the Kyoto Imperial Palace was worth a visit, with its majestic silk hangings and fine painted screens, and the elegantly landscaped pond garden, Oike-niwa.

It was ten o'clock when Junko and Helen rose to go. Hideko gave Junko a hug and Helen a bow. They walked to the bus stop, and there was finally a hint of oncoming autumn in the air. Junko shivered: she hadn't brought a sweater with her. Helen placed her arm around Junko's waist, trying to provide some warmth.

'What do you think happened to Jesse?' Helen asked.

'Dunno. Remember, Aunt Helen, I hardly know him. Maybe he's a cat burglar or something.'

'Kinda tall for a cat burglar, don't you think?' They laughed, and got on the bus. 'Maybe there'll be a message at the hotel,' she added.

'Yeah.' Junko watched the night go by, and wondered.

They checked for messages on their return to the hotel, but there were none.

Junko kissed her aunt's cheek softly. 'See you in the morning,' she said, and went straight to bed.

40

Sunday morning was the start of Junko's third week in Kyoto. She stood in the shower and wondered where the time had gone.

She was pulling on her jeans when the phone rang. 'Hello?' she mumbled, holding the receiver between her chin and shoulder while she did up the zip. There was a lot of crackle on the line and Junko couldn't understand what was being said. 'What?' she raised her voice. 'Hello?'

The line went dead. Junko stared at the phone as if it might explain, but it didn't. *Jesse?* she wondered, and then put the idea out of her mind. She went and knocked on her aunt's door.

Helen was reading the *International Herald Tribune*. 'Breakfast?' She peered over her reading glasses at Junko. 'You ready?'

They ate, and decided to go to Kiyomizu Temple in eastern Kyoto. It wasn't far from Okutan, and the long narrow lane leading up to the temple, jammed with craft and gift shops, was worth exploring further. 'Teapot Alley', Westerners called it. Kiyomizu-zaka was its name.

'Let's go to the temple first,' Helen suggested. 'We can take our time walking back down.'

'Kiyomizu-dera is Kyoto's most celebrated site. It is dedicated to the eleven-faced Buddhist deity Kannon,' Junko read from the brochure.

'It's fantastic!' Helen said. The main hall was perched ingeniously on top of a cliff, on a massive framework made of 139 wooden pillars. The veranda overlooked a steep valley, and the view was broad and breathtaking.

On a second cliff, the sacred Otowa Waterfall dropped down into a courtyard. People were lining up to walk under the water. There were long-handled ladles, and Junko and Helen saw people scooping up the water and drinking.

'Holy water,' a cheerful Japanese woman said, tilting her head towards the falls. 'For good fortune, and long life.'

'*Arigato*,' Junko thanked the woman, and they all got in line. 'I'll drink to that,' she said to Helen, and the Japanese woman smiled.

'American?' she asked.

'*Hai*,' Junko answered.

'Can you eat Japanese food?'

'I like it very much,' Junko said.

The woman frowned. 'Sushi? Can you eat sushi?'

'I haven't tried it yet.'

The woman recovered her smile. 'Ah, so,' she said, nodding with satisfaction. 'Japanese food is very difficult for Americans.'

They drank the water, which was cold and sweet. Then Junko and Helen went to the main hall — a National Treasure, according to the brochure. They took their shoes off before entering the tatami-matted room, and stored them on the shelves provided for this purpose. It reminded Junko of a bowling alley.

The dim hush and the glitter were mesmerizing. And so many people, making prayers and wishes in reverent silence. When Junko thought of wishing, Jesse came to mind, and she pushed the thought away.

They went back out into the sunshine and made their way down the cobbled Kiyomizu-zaka. They were offered free samples of a variety of sweets and cookies from the shops they passed. At one o'clock, Junko said, 'I think we'd better try some sushi, don't you?'

They found a little restaurant called Sushi Kyubey. They started with wild mushroom soup, then moved on to a platter of squid, tuna, eel and salmon, all raw, with some cooked prawns and tiny rice rolls with cucumber in the middle. It was delicious, both women agreed. They toasted their success with green tea.

As they meandered back down the lane, it started to rain. They bought a golden umbrella with autumn leaves swirling all over it and caught a bus back to the hotel.

It was four o'clock, and Helen went to her room for a nap. Junko decided to go to the bookshop for something new to read. She walked along the street with her umbrella open, but the rain softened, and then stopped altogether. In closing it, she accidentally caught a man's shoulder. He was furious.

'*Gaijin*,' he roared, shaking his fist and saying a lot more that Junko couldn't understand. He was a tiny old man, with one eye gloopy, like a mass of cataracts. His good eye glared as he raved at Junko, and his dark business suit strained at his chest. Junko was certain the buttons would fly off like Popeye's.

'*Sumimasen*,' Junko repeated several times, 'I'm really, really sorry.' But the man paid no attention. '*Gaijin*,' he said a last time, with utter disgust, then spat at her feet and walked away.

Junko turned quickly and went back to her room.

41

The summer Junko Bayliss turned six, her mother was fiercely menopausal. Diane believed that she'd never been right since the child's birth; having Junko had drained her of her womanhood. Now, with hot flushes rolling over her in waves and night sweats depriving her of sleep, she was ratty and exhausted, and going mad.

There had been nine cases of encephalitis so far that summer, too. The deadly disease was carried by mosquitoes, and people were warned to cover up when outside, and make liberal use of insect repellents.

On the day of Junko's birthday, Peter was at work. Diane, nerves frazzled, suggested that she and Junko go to Armand Bayou that afternoon. It was a nature reserve, and there were armadillos and snakes and big turtles to see, and sometimes even an alligator or two. Junko loved it there, and was delighted. Was this a birthday treat, she wondered?

'Let's dress up,' Diane said, pushing her limp hair back off her forehead, which was dripping with perspiration despite the air-conditioning. 'Why don't you wear that yellow sundress, and your plastic flip-flops?'

It is a special occasion, Junko thought excitedly as she hurried to get ready. *Mother's treating me!*

When Junko came out of her room, Diane was waiting, tapping her foot nervously and smoking a cigarette. 'Do you want to wear some of my perfume?' she asked, holding the bottle above Junko's head.

Junko nodded dumbly. Her mother never let Junko near her dressing table, especially the perfume. What was going on?

Diane dotted the scent up and down Junko's bare arms and legs. 'There!' she said frantically. 'All done! Now you go on and wait outside for me. I'll be right there.'

Junko went out the back door, and Diane sprayed herself all over with Cutters repellent.

There was only the one attendant at the bayou that day, and no other customers but Junko and Diane. 'One adult and one child, please,' Diane said as sweetly as she could manage.

'Better wrap her up some,' the woman said with a nod in Junko's direction. 'There are more mosquitoes per square foot here than anywhere in Houston.'

'Yes,' Diane replied tersely, the smile still frozen on her face. They entered the park and started walking along the wooden pathway into the trees.

224

'Look!' Junko said when they'd gone no more than a hundred yards. She was pointing at an old hollow log. Playing in front of it were four young armadillos. Their mother was sleeping in the shade near by, doubtless with one eye open. 'Ouch!' Junko said, slapping at her arm, and 'Ouch!' again. Diane's eyes were desperately trained on the armadillos. 'Mother?' Junko said.

'Shhhhh,' Diane whispered. 'You'll disturb them.'

Soon Junko was covered in bites, and itching like crazy. 'Mother,' she pleaded quietly, 'I'm bitten.'

'Let's keep going.' Diane strode forward and Junko wriggled and scratched along behind. They came out of the woods twenty minutes later. They were on the banks of the bayou now, and Junko was near enough eaten alive. She started to cry, and Diane reached into her bag and produced a cardigan. 'Here,' she said without looking at her daughter, 'put this on.'

Junko took the sweater. It was inside-out, and she struggled to turn it around and get her arms in the sleeves. This accomplished, she tried to cover her legs by crouching and covering them with her arms. Just then a mosquito bit her scalp, and she let out a cry.

'Stop that, June. You'll never see an

alligator if you make so much noise,' Diane hissed. Junko was sobbing now, and trying hard to stifle the sound. 'Oh, hell,' Diane said suddenly, 'let's go.' She turned and tramped into the woods and Junko followed.

When they got to the car, Junko was one solid swollen lump of irritation and pain. She climbed in beside her mother, tears streaming down her bitten cheeks but no sound coming from her mouth. Diane couldn't bear to look at Junko, so she didn't. She stared straight ahead and drove them home, thinking, *What have I done?* and *Will it work?* simultaneously. She must be losing her mind.

Back at home, Diane ran a cool bath for Junko, and the girl stayed in it for an hour. When she got out, Diane dotted her all over with calamine lotion and tucked her into bed. Then she went into the kitchen and made some coffee. Peter walked in that evening to find Diane weeping uncontrollably at the kitchen table, and Junko fast asleep.

The next day Peter took Diane to the doctor. Within three weeks she'd had a full hysterectomy and was on hormone replacement therapy. Things calmed down after that.

42

'How about you and I go get some lunch?' Peter was standing at the door to Junko's room with his hands in his pockets. It was twelve-thirty on a windy Saturday afternoon in September, and it looked like a storm could be blowing in. Diane was in the hospital recuperating after her operation, and Peter had taken two weeks off work. Helen could be called on if necessary to look after Junko, but there would be no golf today. Might as well do something different.

Junko was sitting at the desk in her room, drawing. She looked up at her father with a mixture of delight and confusion. She'd never had lunch with just her dad before, and wondered what it would be like. 'Where will we go?' she asked.

'The Blue Clam? You like seafood, don't you, June?'

Junko nodded her head excitedly. 'Do they have shrimp?'

Peter smiled. Junko was a pretty little thing, he thought. Especially when she smiled.

As Peter was backing into the street, a gust

of Gulf wind pushed into the side of the Chrysler New Yorker, and he braked. At that moment their neighbour's cat, Flamingo, flew on to the hood and stood screeching and clawing the windscreen wipers for grip, his fluffy white fur standing on end. Junko gasped and Peter started laughing. The wind subsided and the cat hopped off. They made their way to the restaurant, which was just a few blocks away, with Junko looking anxiously over her shoulder.

'Do you think he's OK?' she asked, unable to see where Flamingo had gone.

'Sure he is. Anyway, cats have nine lives.' He patted Junko's knee. 'He'll be fine.'

'How many lives do people have?' Junko turned back to her father and asked.

'Well,' Peter started, a fistful of grief suddenly punching at his heart, 'depends how you look at it.'

'More than one?'

'Come on,' he said, pulling into a parking space. 'Let's eat.'

They went into the Blue Clam and sat by a window at the back. After the waitress — Darla, her badge said — took their order, Junko asked again, 'Do people have more than one life, Daddy?'

Peter sipped his beer and sighed. 'It's things that happen, June. Sometimes it can feel like a different life.'

'Like Mother's operation? Will hers be a new life after that?'

He shook his head. 'No, I doubt it very much.'

'But she'll get better?' Junko seemed desperate to know. Peter realized with a jolt just what his daughter had been through at the hands of his wife. He'd kept a veil over Diane's doings, especially regarding Junko. But this was too much to ignore. What if, God forbid, her lunatic plan had been successful? He leaned forward and took Junko's hands in his, which made her squirm.

'Sweetheart, I'm so sorry.' His grip slackened.

'Why?' Junko withdrew her hands and put them in her lap. 'Why are you sorry?'

Peter ordered another beer. 'Your mother and I . . . ' he started, but couldn't think of what to say. The food arrived. Junko had a shrimp platter: some broiled, some stuffed, some fried. Peter had the blackened redfish, a spicy Cajun recipe. Both had French fries and breaded okra. Eating kept them silent for a while.

'Daddy?' Junko had eaten all of the fried shrimp first and was holding a French fry in her hand.

'Hmmm?'

'Why are you sorry?'

Peter wiped his mouth and put his napkin on the table. 'June.' He looked hard at his daughter, and found her lovely, for the second time that day. Her white-blond hair was silky smooth, and her pale brow was furrowed with concern. Why did it feel like a revelation? 'Your mother had an accident once, and it was like the end — the end of her first life. *Our* first life.'

'What happened?' Junko's voice was hushed, and her fork slipped from her fingers.

'It was a long time ago. She got, she got sick.'

'Why?'

'God damn it, I wish I knew,' he growled, then held his head in his hands. 'I do know. It was partly my fault.'

'Why?'

'It wasn't *your* fault, that's the thing. It was nothing to do with you.'

Junko was startled, and scared. 'Was I there?'

'No no no no no, you were not. That's the point. It was way before you were born.' The waitress approached them then, asking if they'd like dessert. 'June?' her father asked, and Junko shook her head. 'We'll have the bill, please.'

Their appetites had vanished, so Darla took

the plates away and they stood to go. When they walked outside the sun was shining and the storm had moved on to Friendswood and Alvin. Heat shimmied up from the pavement, and Junko felt more lost than ever. Peter, on the other hand, seemed mightily relieved to be out in the open air.

'Want to go see if Helen's home? I might get a game in after all,' he asked with forced brightness as he held the car door open for his child. They drove to Kemah, and Junko spent the afternoon painting seascapes on the beach with her aunt, who later made Junko's dinner and took her home in time for bed.

43

Junko lay on her bed, trying to recreate in her mind the serene interior of Kiyomizu's main hall. She felt agitated by her cowardice. Why hadn't she just kept going to the bookstore? How had some demented old man made her feel so awful? *The shaking fist*, she thought. *I live in fear of the shaking fist.*

But her parents had never shaken their fists at her. She'd never once been struck by either of them. It was the unspoken accusation that got to her, that she'd done something terribly, terribly wrong and there was no way to atone for it because she didn't know what it was.

She got up and rinsed her face with cold water. The clock at her bedside said 19.30. She was about to go and see what Helen was doing when the phone rang.

'Hello?' she answered, remembering this morning's call.

'Junko? It's Jesse.'

'Hey, Jesse.' Junko feigned lightness.

'I'm in Vancouver. Look — '

'Vancouver? Why?'

'This isn't easy,' Jesse said, after a short pause. 'I got word on Saturday. I had to come. I tried to call you this morning from the airport in Toronto, but I couldn't get through.'

'What happened? Is everything OK?'

'No.' Junko heard a strangled sob. 'My daughter died.'

'Daughter?' Junko felt a wave of dizziness. She put a hand on the wall to steady herself.

'I lied to you.' Jesse was gulping back tears.

She sat down on the edge of her bed. 'Your daughter? What about your wife?'

'No, no. When Abby died, it was complicated. The baby survived, but barely. She had severe cerebral palsy and epilepsy. Marianne.' He choked on the name. 'That's . . . that was my daughter.'

'Oh.'

'Thing is, I couldn't do it, become a full-time carer. I just couldn't face it. She was no more than a lump of flesh and bone. She'd never think or talk or smile. She needed twenty-four-hour care. And,' he wailed here, but briefly, 'she looked like Abby. Exactly like Abby, only with a twisted face.'

'My God. That's terrible. I'm so sorry.' Junko wanted to say something soothing, but she didn't know what, partly because she also felt an overpowering urge to slap him.

'I abandoned her. I flew. My parents went to see her every month, took her stuff, you

know. They were great. I never went at all.'
Junko heard him bang his fist on something.
'God damn it!'

'How old was she?'

'Six. They knew she didn't have much
time, never expected her to live this long.'

'When's the funeral?'

'Tuesday.'

Junko picked at the bedspread, and picked
at words. 'All that stuff about cherry blossoms
and — '

'I'm working on it,' he said. 'I'm still
working on it.'

'I know what you mean,' Junko said with a
deep intake of breath. 'It's OK, Jesse. You did
the best you could. Doesn't sound like it could
have mattered to Marianne much, does it?'

'Wrong.' Jesse's voice was bitter and
emphatic. 'She's the Fat Lady, like Zooey
says, as much as any of the rest of us.'

Junko was nodding her head. She thought
of Yuji, and of her mother, and wanted to
weep. 'Jesse? Why didn't you tell me?'

'I couldn't. Not at first, because it's not
something I tell anyone. And then when I heard
about your folks and Yuji, I thought you'd
hate me.' He paused here. 'Do you hate me?'

'No.' She paused. 'I don't know.' Jesse
groaned. She ran her hand through her hair.
'Are you coming back here?'

'Of course! Junko, I like you. If . . . ' He didn't finish.

'If what?'

'If you want to see me again.'

'When are you coming back?'

'Two weeks.'

'Tell me what time and I'll meet you at the station.'

Junko got Jesse's Vancouver address so she could send some flowers, and they said goodbye. *So, she thought, Jesse is a bit of a liar. Just like the rest of us, I guess. Still, doesn't bode well.*

★   ★   ★

Over dinner in the hotel dining room, Junko told Helen why Jesse had disappeared. Helen sat back, shaking her head. 'Poor man,' she said. 'Men are terrible at coping with these situations.'

'My father managed,' Junko said. 'Didn't he?'

'It's different. And anyway, he didn't cope very well. When I look back, a lot makes sense. Peter was an ambitious but easygoing guy. But as the years passed he drank more and smiled less. Your mother didn't seem to notice, or care.'

'You think he was — what? Bitter about Mother's obsession with Yuji?'

'Maybe.'

'But he came here every year too.'

'He loved your mother deeply. And I'll bet he felt some responsibility for the rape.' Helen drank a sip of beer. 'Incredible. I'm sure he had nothing to do with it.'

'How can you be so sure?'

Helen looked sharply at her niece. 'June, your father wasn't a rapist. I know he let you down big-time, but he wasn't a violent man.'

'No. He wasn't.' Junko could remember wishing he would hit her, instead of blanking her out. A good short whack would have beat a lengthy cold-shouldering any day. 'You want to go for a walk?' she asked Helen.

'Sure. I'll go and get a sweater.'

They walked along the river, watching the gibbous moon bounce on the rippling surface. There was a strong breeze, and Junko was glad she'd put on a heavy sweat-shirt.

'Aunt Helen?'

'Hmmm?' Helen answered, putting her arm through Junko's.

'I think I'm going to stay here for a while. Do the LA work here, and go back to Houston in February to get ready for the show in March. What do you think?'

Helen squeezed Junko's arm tight. 'I think that's marvellous.'

44

After breakfast on Monday morning, Helen went shopping. Junko made her way to Eikando to discuss the use of Toshie's wheel. Timing it might prove difficult. Junko always worked best in the early morning, and she had no idea what Toshie's preference was. Of course, Junko mused, early mornings in Texas were evenings in Japan. Would that affect her rhythm?

'Toshie?' Junko called, tapping on the door, 'it's Junko.'

The door swung open and Yuji stood before her, bowing. '*Imouto*,' he said, and beckoned her in.

'Is Toshie here?'

Yuji handed her a letter in a pale-blue envelope. Her name was written on the front. They sat at the low table and she opened the envelope and began to read.

Dear Junko,
I have to go to Hokkaido for a while. My sister Tami is dying, and I want to be there for her moment of departure from this life, and to help her journey on to the next.

Family members can smooth this transition, you understand?

I want to tell you that you can stay here if you like. I will probably be back for the sakura — that's in the spring. You can use my wheel, and you and Yuji can look after each other, ne? He's a very good cook, in case you didn't know.

Junko, I wish you every good fortune. We are all very glad you came. Wherever you find yourself in the world, you will always have family in Kyoto.

Love, Toshie

Junko folded the letter and put it back in its envelope. She looked at Yuji, who was nodding sagely in her direction. '*Uchi*,' he said with a smile, 'home.'

'Great,' she said dazedly. 'I guess so, anyway.' She stood up to leave. 'Thank you, Yuji. I'll stay at the Royal with Aunt Helen until she leaves next Saturday. Then I'll move in here. OK?'

'*Hai*,' Yuji answered. 'OK.'

Never in all her life had Junko imagined she'd be living in the grounds of a Buddhist temple. It was preposterous! So why did it feel so normal? So inevitable, almost? She walked along the Path of Philosophy shaking her head in disbelief. And with a brother!

HER brother. Would they get along?

'Rivet,' she heard, and stopped. She looked down. A huge frog was sitting in the middle of the path, looking at her. It blinked. Or was that a wink? *Oh my God*, Junko thought, *I'm losing my grip here.* She took a flying leap over the creature and ran the rest of the way to the bus stop.

On the way back to the hotel Junko stopped at the big bookshop she liked. She bought a copy of Basho's *The Narrow Road to the Deep North*, in English and Japanese. Maybe she should try to learn some proper Japanese. Jesse had said it was tough. There were three Japanese alphabets: *kanji*, the Chinese characters, and two of Japanese origin, *hiragana* and *katakana*. Confusing, but worth a try.

She went to Starbucks and got a large latte and a sandwich. She took them to an outside table and opened her book. At the beginning, Basho leaves his home to ramble, but he leaves a poem stuck to a pillar: Behind this door/now buried in deep grass/a different generation will celebrate/the Festival of Dolls.

What a way to travel, Junko thought, *scattering poems behind you. What have I left behind me? Some pots, all breakable. That's about it.*

She drank her coffee and ate her lunch,

then walked back to the hotel. The heat had let up a bit, and there was a breeze off the Kamo-Gawa. Everyone seemed to have slowed down a notch to catch the wind. It was a delightful afternoon.

★ ★ ★

Helen was in her room. She'd bought a silk kimono for Junko, a rich cream colour with a blazing sunrise repeated in embroidery all around the bottom half. Junko tried it on and it felt cool and sensuous next to her skin. 'It's gorgeous, Aunt Helen. I love it.' She gave her aunt a hug. 'What else did you get?' she said, sitting down on the bed and stroking the silk like she would Bodey. She felt a sharp pang of loneliness for her cat. She hadn't thought about Bodey at all when she decided to stay on here. She knew he'd be fine with Gloria and Sharon, but all of a sudden she missed him terribly.

'This is for Molly and Mort,' she said, holding up a beautiful lacquerware box, gold and red and green with inlaid mother-of-pearl and gold leaf.

'It's lovely,' Junko said. 'How are they? I haven't seen them for years, but Molly never forgets my birthday.'

'They're great. Mort's retired, and they

spend a lot of time on their boat in the Gulf. Happy as clams.'

'I've always liked Molly.'

'She's tops all right.'

'Aunt Helen, Toshie's gone to Hokkaido. She says I can stay in her place until the spring. With Yuji.'

'Marvellous!' Helen sat down beside her niece. 'How does it feel?' she asked, taking Junko's hand.

'Well,' Junko replied, 'I'll save a fortune if I move out of this place. I'm burning up my inheritance like wildfire.' She smiled at Helen. 'I kind of like the idea.'

'Come on. I'll help you pack.'

'No.' Junko shook her head. 'I want to stay here till you leave.'

'That's sweet of you, June. I'm glad.'

Junko looked over the rest of Helen's purchases, which included several sandalwood fans, some beautiful handmade paper called *washi*, elaborately decorated pairs of bamboo chopsticks, and a painted paper parasol. Helen had lots of friends.

The two women idled and chattered the afternoon away. Then Junko went to her room for a bath and Helen took a quick nap. They went to a nearby soba bar for dinner, and walked along the river until both were ready for bed.

It had been a good day, and there were four more good days to be had before Helen left. Junko drifted off to sleep with her aunt's voice playing in her ears. 'I think that's marvellous,' she whispered over and over again. 'I think that's marvellous.'

45

Junko's own groaning woke her early. She clutched her belly and got to the toilet just in time to vomit in it. As she stood, she caught sight of herself in the mirror. At that instant she knew she was pregnant.

She stumbled back to her bed and sat on the edge. Tom and Jesse. Both with condoms, several in Tom's case. *Oh my God*, she thought. And then she dressed quickly and went to find a chemist's.

She got back with the pregnancy testing kit just as Helen was coming into the hallway. 'June?' she said when she saw the frantic look in her niece's eyes. Junko unlocked her door and waved her aunt inside.

'I think I'm pregnant,' Junko whispered, as if someone might overhear.

'Pregnant? June, that's wonderful news!'

'But — ' Junko broke off. How could she explain her dilemma to her aunt? And then she thought of her mother never explaining anything. She flopped down on a chair, throwing the bag on the bed. 'Aunt Helen, I've slept with Jesse once. And with another man once, since I've been here.'

'Oh.' Helen sat down across from Junko. 'Ah,' she said.

'Way to go, eh?' Junko said miserably.

'This other man . . . ?'

'Nothing.' Junko shook her head. 'It was just a one-night thing.'

'June — '

'You must think I'm — '

'I think no such thing,' Helen snapped. 'Give me some credit here, June.'

'Sorry,' Junko mumbled into her hair, and started crying. All the desperate sadness, the loneliness and isolation and despair came pouring out in a dam-burst of tears. Helen led Junko to the bed, where she curled up, head in her aunt's lap, and wept. When it was over, Junko sat up and blew her nose several times, then turned to Helen and asked, 'What am I going to do?'

'First off, let's do the test.'

Junko peed in the right place, and confirmed her suspicion.

'OK,' Helen said, stroking Junko's hair. 'Do you want a child?'

'Yes.' Junko's immediate and passionate response took them both by surprise. Junko let out a sigh. 'I guess I do.'

'Right. This baby is your baby, and no one

else's. Fuck 'em!' Junko gaped at her aunt, and they both burst out laughing. 'Or,' she continued, 'you could tell Jesse. He strikes me as a big man in every sense.'

'I don't know. He's just lost his only child. This could . . . it could hurt him a lot.'

'You don't have to decide now. Listen. Why don't you get yourself ready for breakfast, and we'll do some more exploring and let this sink in. OK?' Helen pushed the hair back from Junko's brow.

'I'll take a shower.'

'I'll wait in my room.' Helen stood and went for the door.

'Aunt Helen? Would you mind waiting in here?'

Helen smiled. 'Of course not.' She sat back down and got her Kyoto guidebook out of her bag. 'I'll see where we could go today.'

Junko went into the bathroom and closed the door, knowing her aunt would be there when she got out.

★ ★ ★

They were just finishing their breakfast when Yuji walked into the dining room. He sat down at their table and gave a nodding bow to each of them.

'*Konichiwa*,' Junko said.

'Good morning, Yuji,' said Helen.

They looked quizzically at him. He must have a reason for coming.

'Please come with me.' He stood, and they followed him out of the hotel to the bus stop. Before long they were at Eikando, climbing up a steep path behind Toshie's house.

They came to a level bit of ground where there was a hole dug into the side of the hill. '*Anagama*,' Yuji said.

'Ahhhh,' Junko said, smiling broadly. 'It's Toshie's kiln. An anagama kiln.'

'What's that mean?' Helen asked.

'It's the oldest type of kiln in Japan. They're built into a slope, usually, like this one, and the wood firing takes a lot longer, but you get this natural ash glaze as a result. Beautiful stuff.' She turned to Yuji, who placed a hand on her belly and beamed. '*Akambo*,' he said, and then started making his way down the hill.

'Thank you, brother,' she called, and he turned and waved then carried on.

'Doesn't miss a trick, does he?' Helen laughed. Junko watched until Yuji was out of sight. 'Have you used one before? This kind of kiln?'

'Only once, in college. Sometimes a firing can take weeks. But it's a kind of ritual.' Junko was poking around in the dirt now. 'The college arranged this three-day firing event, when I was a sophomore, and we all put something in. It was exciting, but slow. I got used to quicker results.'

'Will this suit you, then?'

'Oh, yes.' She wiped her hands on her jeans. 'It'll be a whole new slant on things. Let's go, Aunt Helen. I'll check it out later. I've got lots of time.' They started back down the hill. 'A change will be good.'

'And lots of changes will be even better?' Helen asked gently.

'Maybe.' Junko sighed. She wasn't absolutely sure.

They ran into Hiromi on their way through the grounds. '*Konichiwa*,' she said brightly. 'How are you today?'

'Fine, thanks. Yuji's just shown us Toshie's kiln,' Junko replied.

'Ah, so. You will be moving in soon? To Toshie's house?'

'When Aunt Helen goes. She's leaving on Saturday.'

Hiromi nodded. 'It will be good to have you here with us for a while.' Hiromi's warmth was remarkable. Junko felt bathed in it.

'*Arigato*. Maybe I'll learn some Japanese!'

'I think you will learn many things,' she said, placing her hand on Junko's cheek for just a second. 'See you later!' And she hurried off to the gift shop.

46

The days seemed to vanish in a pleasant haze of temples and talks and noodle stalls. Chie was there on Thursday, and spent the evening with them. She told Junko that she'd come off the pill, and was going to try for a child. Junko didn't feel ready to share her pregnancy with Chie; Jesse didn't even know. And, anything could happen. Besides, it didn't feel quite real yet.

'I've got news, too,' Junko told Chie over dinner in the hotel. 'I'm gonna be staying for a while. At Eikando.'

'Eikando? But how?'

'Toshie, who I guess you'd call my sort-of aunt several continents removed, has gone to Hokkaido to be with her sister. She's offered me her room, and her wheel. I'm going to do some work here.'

'You'll stay with Yuji?' Chie asked.

Junko nodded.

'He seems very pleased,' Helen said, and the three women laughed.

'So am I,' Junko added. 'And we can see each other whenever you're here.' She gave Chie's arm a squeeze. 'How about that?'

Chie raised her beer. 'Here's to whatever!' she piped, and they drank.

★　★　★

On the night before Helen was to leave, Junko took her to the Sakura karaoke bar, hoping Tomoyuki wouldn't be there. Or was she? Maybe deep-down she wanted another look at him — just a look.

The room was crowded when they arrived, and they had difficulty finding seats. Finally, a gaggle of chattering office ladies pushed over and let them squeeze in. They ordered Kirin beer, and watched a man sing 'My Way' with the passion of Sid Vicious but the voice of a strangled cat. As he was reaching his unavoidable climax, a face swam into Junko's view. It was Tomoyuki.

'Do you come here often?' he asked with a wink and a grin.

'Every chance I get,' Junko replied with a nervous titter, feeling suddenly afraid. 'Tomoyuki, this is my Aunt Helen.'

'Call me Tom,' he said with a little bow. 'Pleased to meet you.'

'Pleasure,' Helen replied.

'Are you staying long in Kyoto?'

'I have to leave tomorrow, unfortunately. It's a lovely place.'

Tomoyuki eyed Junko, who was trying to talk herself out of the fear she was feeling. *He'd run a mile at the thought of a child*, she thought, *a million miles, probably.* 'You OK?' he asked. Junko was unconsciously clutching her belly.

'What? Oh, yeah. Fine, thanks.' She reached for her glass, wishing he would leave.

'Want to catch a movie some time?' he asked, arching an eyebrow in Junko's direction.

'Uh . . . ' Junko was panicking. 'I've got some work to do right now.'

'I'll call you. Room 418, isn't it?'

Oh my God, Junko thought. *He was actually paying attention.* 'Uh-huh,' she said, looking over his shoulder. She was checking out tomorrow, and a good thing too.

'Nice to meet you,' he said to Helen, and 'I'll give you a ring,' to Junko, before slithering off in the direction of the bar.

Junko breathed out a sigh of relief, and put her glass on the table. Helen looked amused. 'Well, I can see the attraction,' she said, patting Junko's hand. 'You've got nothing to worry about, June. That man hasn't got the slightest interest in fatherhood.'

'But don't men get kind of territorial about kids? Children as property, that kind of thing?'

'They can't if they don't know they've got any!'

Junko looked alarmed. 'Aunt Helen, is it fair? Is it fair to Tom if I don't tell him?'

'June-bug,' Helen leaned in close, her voice intense, 'women have been bringing babies into this world for ever, with or without the help and support of men. Except in the very first instance, of course.' She smiled. 'This is your baby, first and foremost, and if you want to share parenthood, pick someone who you think would do it well.'

Junko picked up her beer, but put it down again fast. 'Ugh.' Her nose wrinkled at the smell. 'I can't drink this. It stinks.'

Helen patted Junko on the back. 'You'll find coffee getting pretty stinky too. Your body will tell you what to do.'

As they left, a very drunken salaryman was singing 'Bye-Bye Love'. Tomoyuki gave them an exaggerated salute from across the room, and Junko and Helen left the bar laughing out loud.

★ ★ ★

Junko lay on the bed while Helen packed her things. She was catching the *shinkansen* at eight-thirty in the morning.

'I wonder if it's a boy or a girl,' Junko

252

thought aloud. 'Not that it matters. I'll take either. I wonder what Jesse . . . '

Helen snapped her suitcase shut. 'Can you call him?'

'Yeah.'

'There's the phone,' Helen indicated with a nod of her head.

Junko sat up. 'It's the middle of the night in Vancouver. I'll call him tomorrow, after you've gone.' These words brought a stab of love to Junko's heart. 'Aunt Helen, thank you. Thank you for coming, and for being there all these years. I can't imagine what would've happened to me if you hadn't. I've never thanked you, not once.'

'You don't need to thank me, June.' Helen sat down and ran her hand through Junko's silky hair. 'I was just part of the family package.'

'Family,' Junko repeated, hand on her still-flat belly.

'Want to go for a walk?'

They grabbed sweaters and went to the riverside for a final stroll together. The half-moon smiled down like Bodhidharma himself, lighting their way through the dark.

47

'Jesse?' Junko was sitting propped up against the pillows on her bed, holding the telephone in one hand and nervously twisting a lock of her hair with the other.

'Hey, Junko. Everything OK?'

'How was the funeral?'

'Good. My brother came out from Montreal with his partner and kids.' Jesse sighed. 'That helped. And my folks were brilliant.'

'I'm glad.'

'Has Helen left yet?'

'I've just got back from the station. She caught the eight-thirty train.'

'Sad?'

'A little. Jesse, I need to tell you something. I was going to wait till you got back here, but I want you to have some time to think about it before we see each other again.'

'What's this?'

Junko drew her breath in. 'I'm pregnant.'

'Whoa. Are you sure? It's only been, how long?'

'Nine days. I'm sure.'

'Have you seen a doctor?'

'No. I got a testing kit. And I've been sick a few times — remember?'

'It's too early — '

'No. Aunt Helen told me Mother was the same, sick from day one.'

Silence.

'Jesse?'

'I'm here. I just can't believe it! This is fantastic. Junko, I love you — I think I do — and I'll look after you and the — '

'Wait, wait. There's another thing.'

'Yeah?'

Namu Amida Butsu, Junko thought, *Namu Amida Butsu*. 'I slept with someone before you.'

'Junko, we've both done — '

'No. I mean in Kyoto.'

'In Kyoto?'

'Yes.'

'Oh.'

'Someone I don't care about, don't even know, really. It was an accident.'

'You don't *accidentally* end up — '

'You know what I mean. I was drunk.'

'Sounds about right,' Jesse snapped back.

'Uh-huh.' *Miserable. My miserable life*, she thought.

'So,' Jesse started, 'we don't know . . . '

'No.'

Silence.

'We can find out, if you want.' The whirring of the air-conditioning seemed louder than before.

Jesse thought about this and then said, 'How long will that take?'

Without a second's hesitation, acting like a woman who knew what she thought and meant and wanted, Junko said, 'Forget it,' and hung up the phone. She curled herself up into a dark blind ball and went to sleep.

48

Junko checked out of the Kyoto Royal Hotel as soon as she was packed. She got a taxi to Eikando, where Yuji was waiting at the gate. He took her suitcase and they walked to Toshie's house together. The sun was shining but there was a cool breeze shimmering through the trees, and Junko felt a shiver creep up her back. The season was changing.

Toshie's room was small but well lit. There were sliding glass doors, which led to a south-facing side porch that would stay sunny for most of the day. Yuji put Junko's suitcase beside the futon and then left with a beaming smile and a bow. Junko went to the wheel and found clay waiting there, wedged and ready: Yuji's work. She sat down and started kicking.

She remembered her first time on the old kick-wheel in Mrs Carney's art room. She'd been fifteen, tall and gangly and terribly shy. Her first efforts had resulted in lopsided blobs, and she nearly gave up. 'Go on, June. It just takes time,' Mrs Carney had said. So Junko had gone on, and on and on, and here she was, still going.

The clay came to life in her hands. She spun a world, a vision, of earth and air and water, which the fire would burn and cement magically together. She drew on the *kami*, on the hills, on possibility, and from her fingers a pot was born.

49

Junko was working at the wheel two months later when Hiromi came to the door. '*Konichiwa*,' she said with a bow. 'Are you busy?'

'Come on in.' Junko went to the sink and washed the clay from her hands. She took Toshie's apron off and put the kettle on. 'Please,' she said, indicating the table, 'sit down. Tea?'

'No thank you. I won't stay long.' They gathered round the low table, and Hiromi folded her hands in her lap. 'How are you?' she asked with a tilt of her head.

'Fine. OK. Only Yuji's going to make me fat if I'm not careful.' Junko patted her belly. 'He could open a restaurant!'

'Kenichiro might be out of a job, then,' Hiromi smiled. 'I think you're going to get fat anyway, *ne?*'

'There is that.' Junko's embarrassment showed. She was glad to be having a child, that the decision had been made for her. But she felt jilted — unfairly, she knew — and quite alone. Yuji helped, but he wasn't a partner. Junko felt her aloneness now as a bald, staring state, an accusation.

'Junko.' Hiromi reached out and touched

259

her hand. 'You can be proud. Life is sacred, and creating life is a gift from the gods.'

'I know,' Junko said, picking a grape from a bunch on the table. She didn't feel very proud. Her initial euphoria had worn off.

'It will get better, when the baby starts to grow.' Hiromi stood up. 'You'll see.' Junko stood with her. 'I have this for you. *Sayonara*.' Hiromi handed her a letter, bowed quickly and was gone.

Junko examined the envelope. There was no stamp, just her name. Without ever having seen his writing, she knew it was from Jesse. It was from Jesse, and contained information that would affect her future, one way or the other. If she read it. She put the letter on the table and made herself a cup of tea.

When Yuji came home that evening and started to cook their dinner, the letter was still unopened. Junko set the table, leaving the pale blue envelope where it lay. She chopped green onions and put various pickles on plates while Yuji prepared rice and pork cutlets and spicy cabbage.

They sat down to eat, but before taking his chopsticks up Yuji picked up the letter and ripped it open, watching Junko as he did so. Junko's jaw dropped in disbelief. 'Hey, brother,' she managed finally to mutter, 'that's my mail.' She wasn't exactly angry, more dumbfounded. Everyone knew it was worse than highway robbery to open other people's mail.

'*Hai*,' Yuji agreed, unfolding the letter and handing it to her without a glance at its contents. 'Read.'

There was no argument here, and Junko felt deflated. There was nothing to do but read the damn thing, she thought, and so she did:

> *Wet autumn wind*
> *scrawls on the face*
> *of the shivering moon.*

Hi, Junko,
I wrote that one. Basho said this:

> *Friends part*
> *for ever — wild geese*
> *lost in cloud.*

I've been hanging on to words here, and counting days. Or, the reverse.

I'd like to see you. Hope that will be possible.

What about Yasaka shrine, tomorrow at noon? No need to reply — I'll go there anyway.

All the best,
Jesse

Junko looked up from the page to see Yuji eating contentedly, and nodding in her direction. She couldn't help but laugh. *It's a conspiracy*, she thought. *But I guess it can't hurt. Or can it?* A chill ran up her back.

★ ★ ★

The next day she was sitting in jeans and a jacket on the rock where she first met Jesse. She was early; it was quarter to twelve. A group of elderly tourists approached her. Kyoto was always busy at *kouyo* time; the hills were just starting to turn into a blaze of scarlet.

'*Gaijin*,' an old man whispered to his wife.

'*Hai, hai*,' the others whispered in agreement. They seemed almost afraid. Junko tried a smile, but that seemed to alarm them even more. They stared for a minute and then scurried away, shaking their heads.

Jesse was early too. 'How are you?' he asked, sitting down beside her and shading his eyes from the bright November sun.

'OK.' Junko sat up straight and examined her once-again clay-stained fingernails. 'It's good to be working.'

'Coffee?'

Junko shook her head. 'Can't do it. Just the smell makes me sick.'

'Do you want to eat?'

Junko nodded, and they found a little noodle bar nearby.

They ordered food, and sat in silence before Jesse said, 'I'm sorry if I — if you think I let you down.'

'No.' Junko shook her head and leaned forward, resting her chin on her hands. 'I don't expect anything from you. I don't *want* anything from you. This is my life, and my child. She'll have plenty of family to — '

'A girl? You already know it's a girl?' Jesse's whisper sounded harsh.

Junko rolled her eyes in exasperation. 'Of course not. I just don't like saying 'it'.' A bowl of crispy noodles was placed in front of her. '*Arigato*,' she smiled at the waitress, and then took a deep breath, looking warily at the bowl.

Jesse's discomfort grew. 'Still sick?' he asked, eyes on his food.

'Sometimes.'

'Abby was never sick.' He realized the accusation implied in his words, and looked up. 'Sorry.'

They started eating, and Junko said, 'Maybe this wasn't such a good idea.'

'Can't we see each other? Now and then? Just until — '

Junko stood quickly and ran to the toilet.

When she came back, Jesse had finished his meal and paid the bill. 'Are you going to finish?' he asked her.

'Huh-uh.' She shook her head. 'I've had enough.' She put on her jacket and held out her hand. 'It's been nice knowing you, Jesse. *Sayonara*.'

★ ★ ★

Yuji was waiting for her when she got home, not off on his usual rambles. He made tea and they sat on the front steps, gazing at the birth of red in the trees, a dazzling transformation taking place before their very eyes.

50

There's a thirty-seven-year-old woman living in Kyoto with her friend Toshie, her brother Yuji and her three-month-old child. She spends her mornings working at a potter's wheel. The wheel belongs to Toshie, who uses it in the afternoons.

As the wheel spins and the clay is conjured between Junko's hands, the baby sleeps in a basket at her feet, or is tickled and cooed at and taken for walks by her Uncle Yuji, or Aunt Toshie, or Aunt Hiromi, or Uncle Kenichiro, or Aunt Helen when she's around. They are visited regularly by Chie, who is still trying for a child of her own. A large and loving family.

Junko has been working on teapots for a year now, all kick-wheeled and anagama-fired, and is due to finish her Kyoto Series for a show in New York City in November. After that, who knows?

In Houston, another artist works at her easel in oils. Hideko is using Junko's room at the Lone Star Pottery for a year, and staying in Junko's house. Bodey has elected to remain with Gloria and Sharon, but he visits sometimes, as do Hideko's parents, which pleases her immensely. She never dreamed she'd be working in Texas. But then, a lot can happen in a year. Or a day, or a moment.

Wake, butterfly —
it's late, we've miles
to go together.

Basho, trans. Lucien Stryk

We do hope that you have enjoyed reading this large print book.

Did you know that all of our titles are available for purchase?

We publish a wide range of high quality large print books including:
Romances, Mysteries, Classics
General Fiction
Non Fiction and Westerns

Special interest titles available in large print are:
The Little Oxford Dictionary
Music Book
Song Book
Hymn Book
Service Book

Also available from us courtesy of Oxford University Press:
Young Readers' Dictionary
(large print edition)
Young Readers' Thesaurus
(large print edition)

For further information or a free brochure, please contact us at:
Ulverscroft Large Print Books Ltd.,
The Green, Bradgate Road, Anstey,
Leicester, LE7 7FU, England.
Tel: (00 44) 0116 236 4325
Fax: (00 44) 0116 234 0205